THE DOLLAR-A-YEAR
DETECTIVE

WILLIAM WELLS

THE DOLLAR-A-YEAR
DETECTIVE

A JACK STARKEY MYSTERY

THE PERMANENT PRESS
Sag Harbor, NY 11963

For information, address:
The Permanent Press
4170 Noyac Road
Sag Harbor, NY 11963
www.thepermanentpress.com

Library of Congress Cataloging-in-Publication Data

Wells, William, author.
The dollar-a-year detective / William Wells.
Sag Harbor, NY: The Permanent Press, [2018]
ISBN: 978-1-57962-527-6
1. Serial murder investigation—Fiction. 2. Suspense fiction.
3. Mystery fiction.

PS3623.E4795 D48 2018
813'.6—dc23   2018019005

Printed in the United States of America

For Mary, as always.

"How often have I said to you that when you have eliminated the impossible, whatever remains, however improbable, must be the truth."

—Sir Arthur Conan Doyle's Sherlock Holmes

Boarding Party

A dead calm came over Pine Island Sound, causing the sailboat, a forty-two-foot Catalina sloop named *Joie de Vivre*, heeled over to port on a broad reach, to gradually slow, right itself, and begin to drift.

It was a warm and humid March evening, and the vanishing of the wind that had billowed the boat's white sails and propelled it forward was felt by the man and woman on deck, as if the temperature had suddenly increased by ten degrees.

The man looked up at the starry nighttime sky, as if he might tell, using an ancient sailor's instinct, if the wind would return anytime soon. He stroked his chin and said to his wife, "We can power back to Fort Myers, or wait here awhile longer and see if the wind comes back up."

As they were pondering that choice, the distinctive sound of an outboard motor was heard puttering across the water, heading toward them from the mainland. As the man and woman turned in that direction, the three-quarter moon, no clouds to dull its brightness, illuminated a white-hulled small boat, with red and green running lights, headed toward them.

A Boston Whaler, with its distinctive silhouette and hull logo, the man thought as the boat came closer, its engine slowing, causing the bow to drop down off plane. A pair of dolphins that had been chasing the boat's wake dove beneath the surface.

"Ahoy there!" a male voice called out. "May I come alongside?"

The man looked at his wife, shrugged, turned toward the approaching boat, and, cupping his hands around his mouth to form a megaphone, shouted, "Who are you?" Not that he could prevent the boat from coming alongside, whatever the answer.

Changing the subject like a politician during a debate, the stranger called out, "Saw you drifting and wondered if you needed a tow."

Now the Whaler was about twenty feet off the sailboat's starboard side, the skipper's face clearly visible in the moonlight. He was in his late thirties or early forties, it appeared, and was wearing a black tee shirt and jeans.

The man said to the Whaler skipper: "Thanks, but we're fine." No need to shout now, with the boat alongside, its outboard, a one-fifty horse Yamaha, sputtering in idle. "We've got a motor."

The offer of a tow was odd, the man reflected, given that sailboats as big as the *Joie* had engines, and, if in need of a tow, he'd have called the Coast Guard. Maybe the Whaler guy was a tourist in a rented boat and didn't know any of that, he thought. Lots of them in Florida coastal waters. In their ignorance of all things nautical, they could be a real hazard. Only last year, the couple had rescued a family—husband, wife, teenage daughter, and black lab—who'd strayed out of the channel from Fort Myers Beach to Sanibel Island and run aground on a sandbar in their rented pontoon boat. Not rescued, really, because they were in no danger of sinking.

Just being polite. The depth of coastal Gulf of Mexico waters was deceptive; if you didn't stay in the channel, you could go from a safe depth to two feet or less without knowing it until too late. That kept the Coast Guard and Sea Tow busy.

Plus, the man thought, there was the matter of how the guy in the Whaler had seen the sailboat in the distance, even with its running lights and white masthead light, at least enough to know it was drifting. Curious . . .

"Okay," the Whaler skipper said. "I'm out here fishing. Mind if I come aboard and use your head?" He was standing now, holding a coiled line, awaiting permission to toss it to the sailboat.

Night fishing was not unusual. The couple were experienced boaters and knew well the tradition of courtesy on the sea. Of course the skipper simply could have stood and urinated over the side of his boat. Nonetheless, the man said, "Sure. That'd be fine." No need to overthink the situation.

The skipper tossed the line, which fell onto the sailboat's deck near the man's feet. He picked it up and looped a section around a cleat using a cleat hitch, tugging to secure it.

"Thanks," the skipper said. "Afraid I drank too much beer."

He stepped aboard the sailboat, a one-man boarding party, and walked toward the couple, who were standing in the cockpit. He stopped three feet from them, took a black pistol out of the belt on his jeans, jacked a shell into the chamber, leveled the pistol at the couple, and said, "Do you recognize me?"

But even if one or both of them did, now that he was closer, all they could see was the gun.

"It doesn't matter," the gunman said, smiling. "Let's go below and have a little chat."

1.

Livin' the Dream

In my experience, many cops share a common retirement dream involving living on a boat in the tropics, like Sonny Crockett in *Miami Vice*, maybe owning a bar with one of those thatched tiki huts on the beach (think wet-tee-shirt contests) and, if divorced, as many cops are (an occupational hazard of the job), dating a beautiful woman who tolerates his flaws and appreciates his good qualities, hidden as they may be.

I'm talking about male cops here. I don't know about the retirement dreams of female cops. If Freud was clueless about what women want, as he famously declared, then how could a guy like me have the faintest idea? The caveat is, sometimes a woman will tell you, with a high degree of specificity, what she wants, and you are well-advised to pay close attention if you want the relationship to continue beyond that conversation.

My name is Jack Starkey and I *am* livin' the dream. I reside on a houseboat named *Phoenix* in Fort Myers Beach, on Florida's Southwest Gulf Coast, where I have lived since moving from Chicago a few years ago, following my retirement as a homicide detective. I own a bar called The Drunken Parrot, and I date a lovely Cuban-American woman named Marisa Fernandez de Lopez. "There are no second acts in American lives," F. Scott Fitzgerald wrote. He was wrong.

For most of the year, the 16,300 year-round residents of Fort Myers Beach, plus the seasonal people and the tourists, coexist reasonably peacefully. But every March, flocks of Girls-Gone-Wild spring breakers descend upon the city like buzzards on a gut wagon.

I'm into nostalgia, old movies and TV shows, including the 1960 movie, *Where the Boys Are*, starring Connie Francis and George Hamilton as college students fleeing snow-covered northern campuses for fun in the sun. Perhaps that role was where George's perpetual tan originated. The movie was about spring break in Fort Lauderdale, but it could just as well have been set in Fort Myers Beach.

Spring break is one of those good news/bad news situations. Good, if you own a bar, restaurant, liquor store, tattoo parlor, budget-rate motel, or a shop that rents mopeds, bicycles, surfboards, paddleboards, or Jet skis. Bad, if you value serenity and easy parking and are uninterested in nonstop partying resembling the bacchanals of ancient Rome, but with beer and tequila shots instead of wine.

I fall into both categories. My party-hearty days are long gone, but about 20 percent of my bar's annual revenue comes in when all those young men and women arrive in search of suds, sand, sun, and casual sex. The Parrot has the suds. Sun and sand are right outside the door. For sex, they're on their own—as long as they don't do it in the Parrot's restrooms (it's happened; now we have a sign in there for patrons saying *no tener sexo*, right beside the one for employees saying *lave las manos*).

It's a Wednesday night during the second week in March. The Parrot is crowded with revelers whose IDs say they are at least twenty-one years old. Undoubtedly some of those IDs are fake, but my bartender, a Seminole named Sam Long Tree, is good at spotting the pretenders and offering them a nonalcoholic beverage or showing them to the door.

Sam is well named. He's as large as a giant sequoia; his suggestions to behave or depart are usually followed without objection. For those who don't comply, Sam gets as physical as necessary. You'd be better off arguing with a speeding bus. He also keeps an aluminum baseball bat and a shotgun behind the bar in case . . . well, just in case.

It's ten P.M., and the cash register is singing a happy tune, accompanied by the blues guitar riffs of Buddy Guy playing loud on the sound system. Undoubtedly our young patrons would rather hear Jay Z, Rihanna, Adele, or Adam Levine, but I own the place. The music of old Chicago bluesmen is what *I* like, so the customers can either accept it, or take their business to another establishment.

I'm in the kitchen, chatting with my short-order cook, a former Marine Corps mess sergeant named Alice Rosewater who's learned to scale back her recipes to serve our customers instead of an infantry battalion. Once Alice caught one of our suppliers overcharging us and threatened to "cut off his head and shit down his neck" if he didn't immediately give us a refund credit. He did. I was a marine, too, so that wasn't the first time I'd heard that persuasively graphic phrase. Said it myself sometimes to underscore a point, back in the day.

Sam finds me in the kitchen and tells me that Cubby Cullen has come in looking for me. Clarence "Cubby" Cullen is the Fort Myers Beach police chief. His nickname immediately called to mind my favorite baseball team. He is short and stocky as a fireplug, with a grey crew cut and a substantial beer belly.

Cubby is a former deputy chief of the Toledo Police Department. When he retired, he and his wife, Millie, bought a cozy little bungalow on a golf course in Fort Myers. For the first year or so, Cubby spent his days fishing and playing golf while Millie tended her garden and played bridge with a regular group of lady friends. That was the retirement life they'd always imagined for themselves. Cubby kept his subscriptions to a number of law enforcement magazines. When he noticed an ad for the chief's job in Fort Myers Beach, he realized how much he missed the cop life. With Millie's blessing, he applied, got the job, and had been running the department for eight years when we met during a poker game at the VFW hall (Cubby had served as an army MP in his younger days).

I find Cubby standing at one end of the bar, watching a young man with one of those three-day growths of beards and Oakley sunglasses perched atop his head, pouring beer from his glass onto the chest of a pretty blonde girl whose Iowa State tee shirt has become transparent, revealing that she must have left her bra back in Iowa.

I think that wearing sunglasses on top of your head is a silly affectation which, for some reason, annoys me, especially when it's nighttime, and sunglasses are clearly just a fashion accessory.

Sam comes out from behind the bar, hands the girl a Drunken Parrot tee shirt, and offers her the option of changing or leaving. She heads to the ladies' room while Sam guides the young man toward the door, his hand on the back of the fellow's neck. I hear Sam ask the kid if he's driving or needs a taxi (Uber hasn't hit Fort Myers Beach yet). He says no, he can walk to his motel, and off he goes, most likely headed to another bar.

Cubby is wearing a Toledo Mud Hens tee shirt (the Mud Hens are the Triple-A Farm team of the Detroit Tigers) and jeans, and not his police uniform, so his arrival has not caused underage drinkers to bolt for the door like undocumented aliens during an INS check.

"Buy you a drink, Cubby?" I ask him.

"No, tonight—I'm on duty," he responds.

His usual is a Blue Moon Ale with an orange slice. My drink these days is Berghoff diet root beer, made in Chicago. I've been sober for the past nine years. It was a gunshot to the left shoulder that caused me to retire from the Chicago Police Department; it was my drinking, plus the additional stress that the cop life brought to my marriage, that led to my divorce, a stay in a rehab center in Minnesota, and then my move to the Sunshine State in search of a new venue, which, I hoped, would start a new chapter in the life of Jack Starkey. So far, it has.

"You're on the late shift tonight," I tell him.

"I was home watching *Blue Bloods* on TV when I got a call from the duty officer at the station. The Coast Guard reported they'd found a sailboat drifting in Pine Island Sound with two bodies aboard, a man and a woman. Both shot in the head."

"Where's the sailboat now?"

"It was towed to the Coast Guard station on San Carlos Island."

"Have you been aboard?"

"I'm on the way. I'd like you to take a look at the crime scene. No one in my department has the kind of experience with homicides that you do."

"Sure, glad to help if I can," I tell him.

I don't know who coined the proverb, "No good deed goes unpunished." But whoever it was got it right, in spades, as I was soon to find out.

2.

One Crime Scene Too Many

We take Cubby's white Ford police SUV north across the San Carlos Boulevard causeway to the US Coast Guard Station on San Carlos Island. The station is a three-acre compound surrounded by a sixteen-foot chain-link fence topped with razor wire. We pull up to a guard gate manned by a petty officer in a blue uniform, wearing a sidearm. The guard asks to see Cubby's ID. He shows his badge; the guard looks at me and says, "And who are you, sir?" Cubby tells him I'm helping with a police matter and the guard waves us through the gate.

We drive past a two-story cinder-block building with a flagpole out front; on it, an American flag is unfurled and illuminated by three spotlights set into the concrete around the pole, with a Coast Guard flag hanging beneath it. I know from my days in the Marine Corps that, after sunset, you either have to take down an American flag or light it up.

Cubby parks in a lot near a long concrete pier. A Fort Myers Beach police squad car, an unmarked brown Crown Victoria, a crime scene van, and an EMS vehicle are also parked there. The Crown Vic belongs to one of Cubby's detectives. I always wonder why police departments think that brown sedans with black walls and whip antennas can pass as civilian cars, but law-enforcement fleet management is above my pay grade. The FBI is partial to black Suburbans that shout, "Here come the Feds!" If a perp is dumb enough to be fooled by either kind of vehicle, he deserves to be caught.

Cubby and I get out of the SUV and walk out onto the pier. When I arrived in Florida, I didn't know the difference between a pier and a dock. Samuel Lewandowski, who owns Salty Sam's Marina on Estero Bay, where I keep my houseboat, informed me that a pier is a dock big enough to allow vehicles to drive on it. If that question ever comes up in a trivia contest, I'll be on it like Ernie Banks on a fastball down the middle.

The eighty-seven-foot-long cutter *Valiant* is moored on one side of the pier. By tradition, the Coast Guard calls its vessels "cutters." On the other side, a big sailboat with a blue hull is tied up, and behind the sailboat is a Coast Guard SAFE boat—that's a small aluminum craft with a cabin and twin 350-horsepower Mercury outboards. It probably was the SAFE boat that towed the sailboat to the station.

The name painted on the stern of the sailboat is *Joie de Vivre*. How ironic that a vessel whose name translates as "joy of life" contains two dead bodies.

A uniformed police officer and an EMT tech in white coveralls are standing on the pier beside the sailboat. They are both regulars in my bar. The uniform is a tall man with black hair and a chiseled jaw in his late twenties named Brad Jennings, and the EMT is Caroline Jackson, an African American woman in her thirties.

I greet them by name. Cubby and I step aboard the sailboat. As we do, a man appears out of the companionway leading to the cabin: he is a veteran Fort Myers Beach

detective named Harlan Boyd. Boyd is heavyset, in his fifties, with thinning brown hair, the bent nose and scar tissue
under his eyes of a former boxer, which he is, and the florid
complexion of a man who is not unacquainted with strong
drink, which he frequently finds at my bar. We give discounts
to law enforcement officers, as well as to military personnel,
active duty and retired. One elderly gent who is a regular
landed at Omaha Beach in WWII. He drinks for free.

Boyd is wearing a suit and white rubber surgical gloves.
He also is wearing a grim expression. I say: "Hey, Harlan."

He nods at me and says, "Jack." Then he looks at Cubby,
shakes his head and says, "This is a bad one, chief."

When a veteran detective says it's a bad one, it's a bad
one.

Boyd pulls a handkerchief from his pants pocket and
mops sweat from his forehead. It's a warm evening, but not
warm enough at that hour to cause someone to perspire that
much—unless he's just seen something he'd like to un-see.

On the way over, Cubby assured me he'd told Boyd I was
coming, and that Boyd doesn't mind if I check out his crime
scene. Some detectives are very territorial, some less so. I was
in the "very" category when I was a homicide detective in
Chicago.

Boyd hoists his bulk onto the pier, pulls a pack of cigarettes from his inside jacket pocket, taps out an unfiltered
Camel, fires it up with a Zippo, takes a long drag, and lets
thin white strands of carcinogenic smoke waft out of his
nostrils.

"The CSIs have done their bit and left," he tells us. "Linda's inside." He means Linda Evans, the Medical Examiner's
crime scene tech.

"Why'd this damn sailboat haveta drift into *my* fucking
jurisdiction?" Boyd asks, rhetorically. "A few miles north,

and it's Cape Coral's problem. Few miles south, and Bonita Springs catches the case . . ."

If I were a Fort Myers Beach detective, I think I'd be happy to have some action to test my skills. But not Harlan Boyd, apparently.

Cubby and I descend three steps into the cabin, move through the salon and into the galley. The *Joie de Vivre* is a luxury yacht and well-appointed. All brass and mahogany. First class all the way. In comparison, the houseboat I live on is a garbage scow—but it's *my* garbage scow.

Linda Evans has short brown hair and round, wire-rim glasses that give her an owlishly studious appearance. She joined the department a year earlier after getting a master's degree in forensic science from Florida Gulf Coast University. Before that, she was a police officer in Bradenton.

Linda is wearing blue coveralls that say "Crime Scene Tech" in white lettering on the back. She is squatting down, tying a plastic bag onto the right hand of a man lying on his back. He is, or was, a handsome man in his mid-to-late forties, I guess, with dark brown hair. I estimate that he is about six feet tall when vertical, which he never will be again. He's wearing a blue-and-white striped tee shirt, tan canvas shorts, and boat shoes—typical sailors' garb. There is a bullet wound in his forehead, apparently from a small-caliber handgun, from the size of the entrance wound. His eyes and mouth are open, giving him the expression of a man who'd been surprised by something—presumably by being shot in the forehead.

"You know Jack Starkey," Cubby says to Linda. "He'll be consulting with the department on this case."

Consulting. First I've heard of that. I thought I was just taking a look. Cubby and I will have to talk.

Linda looks up at me, nods, finishes bagging the dead man's hand, then does the other one and stands up. DNA from the killer might be found under the dead man's fingernails, or elsewhere, but that seems unlikely because there is no sign of a struggle. If the gunman has any brains at all, he didn't get close enough to his victim for that. That's the point of having a gun.

Bedrooms on boats are called berths. Bathrooms are called heads. Kitchens are galleys. Floors are decks and walls are bulkheads. Doors are hatches. Rope is line. The front of the boat is the bow, the rear is the stern, the right side is starboard, and the left is port. All of this from Salty Sam, who told me I should know nautical terms, "In case you ever get a real boat." Ha ha.

Sam spent thirty years in the Merchant Marine before opening the marina where my houseboat is permanently moored (the previous owner didn't list "seaworthy" as one of the boat's amenities). I named my boat *Phoenix* after the bird of Greek mythology that rises from its own ashes, as I hoped to do by starting a new life in Florida. Sometimes, when I have a guest aboard, I show off my nautical knowledge by saying, "If you need to use the bathroom, you'll have to go ashore. All I have is a head."

The woman on the bed in the master berth looks younger than the man, maybe in her thirties, with short dark hair and sightless blue eyes. She is lying on her back on top of the covers with a bullet wound similar to her husband's in her forehead. She is wearing a black halter top and white shorts.

"Okay, that'll do it," Cubby says, more to himself than to me, his "consultant."

We go back onto the pier, where Harlan Boyd is finishing his smoke. He takes a last puff and flips the butt into the water. A fish rises, noses it, and submerges. Not his brand.

We're standing beneath a clear sky and a luminescent, three-quarter moon. The lights of Sanibel Island are visible across the twelve-mile stretch of Gulf of Mexico water: a lovely night to be alive, which the victims on the boat are not.

Boyd runs his fingers through his hair, looks at the *Joie de Vivre*, which had been transformed from a pleasure cruiser into a crime scene, and asks me: "This why you retired, Jack? Dealing with this kind of thing?"

"Mainly it was getting shot, Harlan."

"Never been shot," he says. "Shot *at*, but not hit. So far."

"Continued good luck with that. It can really ruin your day."

Cubby asks Boyd: "What'd the Coast Guard say?"

"A fisherman called in a report of a sailboat drifting in Pine Island Sound, about seven o'clock. The Coast Guard sent out a boat with two crewmen, that SAFE boat there. They located the sailboat, hailed it on the radio and then with a megaphone, and got no response."

He pulls a notebook out of his inside sport coat pocket, flips it open, studies it for a moment, and continues: "Petty Officer Second Class Robert Michaels boarded the sailboat while Master Chief John Pulaski remained aboard the SAFE. Michaels rigged a towline, then went into the cabin and found the bodies. He vomited into the galley sink, went back aboard the SAFE, told Pulaski what he'd found, and Pulaski radioed it in. He was told to record the location and tow the sailboat here."

He looks at his notebook again. "Michaels wasn't wearing gloves, but he said he didn't touch anything. The Coast Guard duty officer, a Lieutenant Jeffrey O'Neil, called the department at 9:42. Patrolman Tom Breckenridge was closest in his squad and got here at 9:50. I got here at 10:10. Not that the timing matters one iota to the vics." He closes the notebook and says, "That's all we got so far."

"Any ID on them?" Cubby asks.

"According to their Florida driver's licenses, the man is Lawrence Henderson and the woman, presumably his wife, is Marion Henderson. They reside at 2010 Royal Palm Circle in Cape Coral. We'll get the names of next of kin in the morning. The boat is registered to Lawrence. I Googled him. He's president of Manatee National Bank in Fort Myers."

Boyd takes the pack of Camels from his inside coat pocket, taps out another cigarette, lights it with the Zippo, takes another long pull, tilts his head toward the sailboat, and asks, "Now who'd do something like that, for chrissakes?"

"What we need to find out, Harlan," Cubby answers.

Harlan responds: "Not a robber, because no valuables were taken. It probably was someone who knew the Hendersons, knew that they would be on their boat, where the boat would be, and when. I'll try to find out where they kept the boat, and if anyone saw anything before the Hendersons set sail."

So Harlan Boyd knows his stuff. I wonder why Cubby thinks he can't handle this case on his own—if he doesn't die of emphysema or lung cancer first. He says: "My brother Frank's got his own insurance agency up in Jacksonville. Life, auto, homeowners. Does real well. Nice house, nice car, nice family . . ."

He shakes his head.

"Things like this make me think I should go into the insurance business with Frank. He says I can, anytime I want. I've thought about doing that in a few years. But maybe now's the time."

He takes another hit on the Camel, flips it into the water—no interest from the fish this time—and continues: "Best thing about being in the insurance business? Frank's never seen a dead body except in a funeral home. Whole different deal from police work."

"I hear you, man," I tell him.

Cops reach the end of the line at different times and for different reasons. Some put in their thirty and retire reluctantly. Some burn out earlier; maybe they're the ones who care too much. This crime scene is bad, but nowhere near the worst I've seen.

But, for whatever reason, Detective Harlan Boyd apparently has seen enough of them. I'm going below again to take a better look at the scene for myself.

3.

Once a Detective, Always a Detective

Cubby and I ride in silence back to my bar. Not having seen a dead body with a bullet hole for a while, I'm thinking about guns and the debate over the meaning of the Second Amendment now happening in the country.

A gun, by itself, is an inanimate object, a mechanical device, a machine made of steel, plastic, composite materials; all slides and levers and chambers and bores and springs, a complex tool engineered to produce a controlled explosion that sends a lead projectile at supersonic velocity toward a target. Sometimes the target is inanimate: a paper target in a shooting range, or a bottle or can set atop a fence. Sometimes it's a living thing, a person or an animal.

But a gun, by itself, is incapable of performing the task for which it was made. For that it needs a human operator. Be it a handgun or long gun, an ancient cannon, a big-bore behemoth mounted on a naval vessel, or a tank or ground emplacement, a gun cannot feel emotions, such as rage, or fear, or the thirst for revenge or the need for self-protection. It takes a person to feel those emotions, and then pull the trigger to unleash the lethal force.

Bad guys will always find a way to have a gun, detectives will always be called upon to chase the shooters, and, as long as the bad guys have guns, I want to have one too. Whether or not limiting the public's access to firearms will reduce gun violence is a hotly debated question. In countries such as England, Japan, and Australia, where firearm owner ship is closely regulated, gun violence is very low. In the US, where firearms are easily obtainable, the gun homicide rate is twenty-five times higher than in other high-income nations.

So: Will restricting gun ownership reduce the chance that some lunatic would walk into an elementary school and open fire, creating a horrific carnage? Or is the best bet to train and arm selected school employees, under the assumption that psychopaths will always find illegal weapons?

I don't know. But someone had somehow acquired a pistol, used it to murder Lawrence and Marion Henderson, and I'm being asked to help find the killer. The debate about the proper interpretation of the Second Amendment is irrelevant to the task at hand. I'll leave the rest to partisans, politicians, cable news talking heads, and Supreme Court justices. That's about as philosophical as I get on the issue. The rest—as I said about law-enforcement fleet management—is above my pay grade.

Cubby parks in front of The Drunken Parrot, turns toward me, and says, "I need you in on this one, Jack. A bank president and his wife were murdered. It's as high profile as a case around here can get. And if you didn't notice, Harlan has pretty much had it. I've seen that before, in Toledo. When someone gets that way, they're no good to the department or themselves. Plus Harlan's wife is pushing him to get a different job, what with all the shootings of cops these days. I expect him to pull the pin anytime."

"You've got two other detectives, Cubby."

"Yeah, Ronnie Patterson and Nick Montez. Good guys, both of them—if your car gets stolen or your boat gets vandalized, or some such. Nick took down a meth lab about a year ago. It was a big deal, but we'd gotten a tip about it. But those guys on this one . . . no way, no how. This is right in *your* wheelhouse."

"Last time you asked me to get involved in a case, chasing that serial killer in Naples, it almost got me killed."

Cubby gives me a knowing look. "Admit it, Jack. You loved the hell out of it. Once a detective, always a detective."

Cubby had introduced me to his friend, the former Naples police chief. Naples is a little city twenty miles to the south of Fort Myers Beach that is one of those playgrounds of the superrich. By the time many, if not most, of those residents arrived, their youth and middle age were in the rearview mirror; Naples, it was said, was a town populated by the elderly, and their parents. That also had begun as a consulting assignment. But soon I was leading an investigation involving a fake Russian count with Mafia ties running a hedge fund named after a sunken Spanish treasure galleon, and three wealthy, self-styled Old White Men, bored in retirement, who began playing dirty tricks on people who annoyed them, and ended up employing a Miami hit man to eliminate people they didn't like. Including me. That was two years ago. I did enjoy the adrenaline rush of the hunt.

"So what's your initial impression?" Cubby asks as I open the SUV's passenger-side door.

I lean back in my seat. "Boyd nailed it. I agree with everything he said."

"So, speaking theoretically, if you were going to handle this case, where would you start?"

"I'd take a theoretical pen and a theoretical legal pad and draw two theoretical columns. The first column would contain the pros of getting involved in your investigation, and the second column would list the cons. I'd start with the pros. After a while, I'd realize that there are no pros, and so it would be irrelevant to list the cons. I'd go back to my happy life as it was before you walked into my bar tonight."

"At least think about it," Cubby says, not looking at me. We play poker with a group of guys at my bar once a week. When Cubby averts his eyes like that, it's a "tell": he's got a good hand.

"Okay, I'll think about it, Cubby," I say.

No harm in that. Or so it seemed at the time.

4.

Stoney's Dilemma

I wake up the next morning aboard *Phoenix*, pad into the galley, hit the brew switch on the Mr. Coffee, slip a strawberry Pop-Tart into the toaster, and open a can of tuna for my cat, Joe.

My houseboat is permanently moored at Salty Sam's. Permanently, as in: it never leaves the dock. It's very comfortable as a residence, cozy in fact, but whenever I go out onto the saltwater to fish, I rent a boat from the marina because it has a better chance than *Phoenix* of not doing a *Titanic* number on me. Sam told me he can't recall the previous owners ever taking *Phoenix* out. It was delivered to the marina on a truck and used as a winter vacation home by a couple from Syracuse. The wife got it in their divorce.

After I'd been living on *Phoenix* for about three months, a large tiger-striped feline with the scars of a street fighter came aboard uninvited. I was happy to have the company and named him after my brother, a Chicago fireman who died trying to save a young boy's puppy from a burning fourflat. The puppy survived but my brother did not.

I sit at the galley table, drink a cup of coffee while watching cable news on the flat-screen TV mounted on the wall (bulkhead), and then pour another cup. I'm not a morning person. Mornings, for me, are like waking up from a long coma. It takes awhile for all of my mental and physical functions to reactivate. That's one reason I didn't make the marines a career. For some reason, they think the workday should begin at zero dark thirty with a fifty-mile hike. Other reasons included sleeping on the ground and getting shot at.

The caffeine kicks in as I finish the Pop-Tart. I walk out onto the deck and pick up my copy of the *Fort Myers News-Press* that the paperboy, on his bicycle, delivers each morning. As I'm reading the sports section, Cubby calls.

"We've got some more on the murders," he tells me. "The Hendersons have two children, an eight-year-old son, Nathan, and a six-year-old daughter, Elise, who were staying with an aunt and uncle on Sanibel Island when their parents were killed during their recreational sail. The coroner's doing the autopsies now. And Harlan's called in sick. Can we get together?"

The fact that the children are safe, amidst the tragedy, is a blessing. Sometimes in this life, the most you can hope for is a positive balancing a negative, a yin balancing a yang, especially in the homicide business, although that's rarely the case.

"Sure, Cubby, as soon as I do something first," I tell him.

"No problem. How about I buy you lunch and I'll brief you."

I know that agreeing to be briefed also means agreeing to consult, which inevitably means taking on the role of lead detective. I haven't made up my mind about that yet. To seal the deal, Cubby says, "Stan's Diner at noon?"

It's a bribe, and it works.

Stan Kowalski is from Chicago. His diner features the cuisine I grew up with: deep-dish pizza, Italian beef and sausage sandwiches, and the famous Chicago-style hot dog—a Vienna beef frank in a poppy-seed bun, topped with diced tomatoes, bright green relish, onion, pickle spears, sport peppers, and mustard. You order ketchup on a hot dog in my hometown and they banish you to Michigan, where they put ketchup on everything, from steak to eggs. Stan's wife, Irene, makes pies so good that they get eaten by the customers before they have a chance to cool off.

"Okay, see you at Stan's at noon," I tell him.

I need to do some work on a literary project this morning. Bill Stevens, a *Chicago Tribune* police reporter I know, writes a series of best-selling crime novels based upon my career as a Chicago homicide detective. He pays me to read through his manuscripts to help him get all the cop stuff right. If, for example, an author writes that a certain gun comes in a certain caliber, and it doesn't, or that Ford's Police Interceptor engine (like the one in Cubby's SUV) has a maximum of two hundred fifty horsepower (it did, but the new engines go up to three hundred sixty-five hp), some readers notice, and get annoyed. In the old days, they might have written a note to the author via his publisher, but now they post their criticisms on social media, for all the world to see.

Bill's fictional detective is named Jack Stoney—not a big leap from Jack Starkey, but I don't mind, even though I get a lot of ribbing from friends about how Stoney has a higher close rate than I do, both with his cases and with the ladies.

I have the manuscript of Bill's new book, *Stoney's Dilemma*. Bill could retire from the *Trib* and just write books, but he says the job keeps his head in the crime game. He is my silent partner in The Drunken Parrot.

I top off my cup of coffee, get the manuscript and a red Sharpie from a galley drawer, and begin to read where I left off a few days ago:

"You say you want a lawyer?" Stoney asked Lonnie Williams *as they sat across at a table in the precinct interrogation room.*

"Sure, that's fine. You can do that. Just like I told you when I cuffed you in that alley. You remember what I told you, right?"

Lonnie Williams didn't answer, just as he hadn't answered any of Stoney's questions about the rape of an eleven-year-old girl snatched from a school playground on Dearborn a week ago. So far, the only evidence against Williams was the word of one of Stoney's snitches, Jake the Snake, who'd traded the tip for a double shot of Four Roses with a beer back at the Baby Doll Polka Lounge. An unreliable witness who a prosecutor would not call to the stand in a courtroom.

So, to make the case, Williams had to admit to the crime. The department had gotten touchy about "enhanced interrogation techniques" ever since the scandal involving a warehouse on the West Side of Chicago known as Homan Square, where perps like Williams could disappear from the public record. Stoney had gotten his share of confessions at Homan, but that was then, and this was now.

"I told you that you have the right to remain silent, the right to an attorney, that anything you say can be held against you in a court of law and all that other Miranda bull crap. So say the word, and we're done here, and you'll obtain the services of some young assistant public defender from a fourth-rate law school who just barely passed the bar exam on his umpteenth try, and who will give you the representation you're paying for, by which I mean zip."

Lonnie Williams averted his eyes and kept on saying nothing. Stoney went out of the room and came back with a plastic evidence bag containing something made of white cloth and slid it across the table toward the suspect.

Williams glanced at it and said, "That supposed to mean somethin' to me?"

"These are your victim's underpants," Stoney said. "I'm betting that the stain on them is from your bodily fluids, proven by a DNA match."

5.

The Dollar-a-Year Man

It's Thursday. That means the pie of the day at Stan's is straw-berry rhubarb, if I remember correctly, one of my favorites. The pies Irene makes on the other six days are my favorites too.

I swing into Stan's lot, which is covered with ground sea-shells called coquina. The building is classic 1950s diner style, looking like a large aluminum Airstream trailer with illumi-nated multicolored neon lights around the roof, sides, and front door.

Cubby, wearing his police uniform, is seated in a booth near the door. The Beach Boys song, "I Get Around," is play-ing on the old-time flashing-neon Wurlitzer jukebox, similar to the one in The Drunken Parrot.

As I slide into the booth, Cubby says, "Let's order, then I'll tell you what I've got."

Miriam, one of Stan's veteran waitresses, comes over and takes our orders for bacon cheeseburgers and fries. My next annual physical is eight months away, so I have plenty of time to get my blood chemistry in order by eating Greek yogurt and kale. But probably not.

Miriam is in her fifties, with reading glasses hanging from a gold chain around her neck, and she's wearing a white uniform with a name tag. I ask Miriam to reserve a piece of the strawberry rhubarb pie for me. Cubby preorders the rice pudding, another popular item. She heads for the kitchen and Cubby says: "The autopsies are still underway, but the coroner reports that the Hendersons died from shots to the head with a .22-caliber pistol from close range."

"Like a pro does it."

"My thought too."

"Meaning it was a planned execution, like Boyd said."

"Looks like it."

He takes a spoonful of pudding. "Can't have a professional hit man roaming around shooting up the citizenry, Jack. Not on my watch."

"I'd say that's bad for property values," I comment.

Cubby looks at me. "I can't pay you as much as they did in Naples. Basically what a detective first grade makes, which is eighty grand a year plus expenses."

I don't need the money, but, I realize, I want to feel . . . *useful* . . . again. "Save your money, Cubby. I'll do it for a dollar a year."

Cubby grins, seeming unsurprised. "Thank you, Detective Starkey. Speaking of money, I assume you'll want to start with an audit of the Manatee National Bank."

Good idea. The number one rule in the *Detecting for Dummies* handbook is: follow the money. Maybe Henderson's bank is laundering drug money. Something went wrong, as drug deals usually do, and it had gotten him and his wife killed.

"I know the special agent in charge of the FBI office in Tampa, which covers Lee County," Cubby says. "Daniel Morrissey. I spoke with him this morning and he offered his full cooperation. The murders fall under our jurisdiction but if Henderson's bank is involved in illegal activity, the Feds have an interest because banks are federally insured."

"Obviously, you assumed I'd take the job," I say.

He just smiles. Our food arrives. Cubby takes a bite of his burger and says, "Stop by my office for your badge and gun."

6.

On the Job Again

The next morning after breakfast, I drive to Fort Myers Beach police headquarters, a two-story brick building on Peck Street. I enter through the glass door, nod a greeting to the desk sergeant, Lenny Warinski, detour into the break room to pick up a cup of coffee and a jelly doughnut, and walk up a stairway to Cubby's office. I could have taken the elevator, but I need to work off the Pop-Tart before I eat the doughnut.

Cubby is seated at his desk, reading a file. A large tarpon is mounted on the wall behind him. I was with him when he caught it in Boca Grande Pass. He looks up and says, "Day one on the job, Jack. Today you'll earn one three-hundred and sixty-fifth of your salary."

"I'll let it ride until it adds up to a quarter."

He opens a desk drawer and hands me the real compensation for the job: a black leather case containing a gold detective's shield. I put it in the front pocket of my khakis, where it feels right at home.

I didn't get a shield while working on the Naples murder case because I was undercover. I'll confess that I've never felt fully dressed since turning in my shield in Chicago. A detective's shield and gun don't come with a license to kill like James Bond had, but they sure come in handy when you're sticking your nose into some bad guy's business.

"Do you want one of our department-issue 9mm Sig Sauers?" Cubby asks.

"Thanks, but I'll go with my Colt."

Meaning the .45-caliber Colt 1911 semiauto that I carried earlier in my life. It saved my bacon more than once.

"Best to stick with an old friend," Cubby says. "So what's first on the agenda Monday morning?"

"I'll drive to Tampa to meet with the FBI. After that, I'll pay a visit to Henderson's bank."

"Be careful out there," Cubby says as I'm leaving, echoing the phrase from one of my favorite TV shows, *Hill Street Blues*.

Cubby is flying to Cleveland this afternoon to attend a funeral. The son of one of his high school friends was a police officer who'd been shot and killed during a routine traffic stop. Part of the daily risk a policeman takes.

So I'm on the job again. *Phoenix* is aptly named. Like the bird of Greek mythology that rose from the ashes, I hoped that my move would help me become a better man. My single-minded devotion to my job as a homicide detective caused me to neglect my family and, as with so many cops, the stress of the job caused me to drink too much. No excuses—many, if not most, cops handle the stress without self-destructing. My wife, Claire, finally had enough of me and the whole package of cop life. She asked for a divorce. I didn't contest it because I wouldn't have wanted to be married to me either, back then.

My retirement from the Chicago PD came not long after I took a .380-caliber round in the right shoulder, through-and-through, that limited my range of motion so badly that I was granted a three-quarters disability and get monthly checks in the mail. Rehab restored my full range of motion, so the joke is on the taxpayers of the City of Chicago. I don't feel badly about that because the pols would waste or steal the money. And because it's the third time I'd been shot, once in the Marine Corps while guarding a United States Embassy in the Middle East, and one other time while on the City of Chicago's payroll. Get shot once, consider it bad luck. Twice, examine your tradecraft. Three times, think about a different line of work.

7.

The Big Kahuna

Tampa is a three-hour drive from Fort Myers Beach on I-75 North. It is a perfect morning, the sun looking like a lemon Necco Wafer in a cloudless azure sky (loved them as a kid), the temperature in the high seventies. Just another routine day in paradise. I have the top down and the radio tuned to a Golden Oldies station playing Bruce Springsteen's "Born in the USA." Perfect tune for a motor trip.

I spent the weekend puttering around the bar and doing some maintenance on *Phoenix*, which mainly consisted of hosing seagull poop off the roof and deck. I did my daily three-mile run on the beach and one hundred push-ups and sit-ups. Back in the day, it was six miles, and two hundred of the rest. You do what you can, right up until the day you find yourself sitting in the day room of the Happy Pelican Retirement Home, drooling oatmeal on your pj's, watching *Judge Judy* reruns and trying to remember if it's bingo night. I hope that day is a long way off.

The FBI's Tampa office is a four-story stone building with a red tile roof, surrounded by a low iron fence on West Gray Street. The architecture, the palm trees on the grounds, and the pond with a fountain on the front lawn give the place a deceptively serene appearance, more like a private residence than a government office building, except for the manned guard gate. Inside, wars are being fought on many fronts: crime, organized and disorganized, drugs, illegal immigration, and terrorism.

I pull up to a gate as a man wearing the blue uniform of the Federal Protective Service, a bulletproof vest, and a sidearm appears from the guardhouse. He is tall and muscular, in his thirties, with a military haircut; he looks like he could pick up my car and turn it around as a sign that I am being refused entry. I give my name, show my detective's badge, and tell him I have an appointment with Special-Agent-in-Charge Daniel Morrissey.

He tells me to wait, goes into the guardhouse, comes out, hands me a cardboard car pass, which he instructs me to display in my windshield at all times, and then goes back into the guardhouse and opens the gate electronically.

There is a convention in crime fiction—novels, TV shows, and movies—that an institutional animosity exists between the Feds and local police forces: jurisdictional disputes, information hoarding, and a negative view of one another's abilities. But, in my experience, this is not the case, having worked with FBI agents, state police detectives, and county sheriff's departments, always with a good result. We were all focused upon tracking down and apprehending the bad guys, especially when we were brought together on an anti-terrorism task force, so I have no apprehension about working with the Feds on this case, or any other.

I find a visitor's spot and leave my Colt locked in the trunk. If you want to stir up some excitement, try carrying a gun into a federal building. I enter through double glass doors and encounter two more uniformed guards manning a security portal like the ones in airports. One of the guards orders me to put my personal items into a basket on a conveyor belt that passes through a scanner and to walk through the portal. The alarm goes off as I do. One of the guards puts his hand on his holstered pistol while the other runs a hand scanner over me. When that produces nothing he has me take off my belt, which has a large metal buckle. I do and walk back through the portal. It was the buckle.

I see an information desk near the elevators. A woman in her twenties, with short dark hair, wearing the same kind of guard's uniform, checks for my name on her computerized visitors' log, then says that Morrissey's office is on the fourth floor. Maybe, when she is off duty, she can gin up a nice smile.

Riding up in the elevator, I wonder if the FBI provides visitors with doughnuts and coffee. Arriving on four, I follow a sign indicating that the Big Kahuna, aka Morrissey, can be found down the hall to the right. I head that way and come to a set of floor-to-ceiling glass doors which have the seal of the Federal Bureau of Investigation on one of them and Morrissey's name and title on the other.

Inside a young woman in civilian clothes sits at a large reception desk; she is typing on a computer keyboard.

"May I help you, sir?" she asks me.

"I'm Detective Jack Starkey. I have an appointment with Agent Morrissey."

She checks a log and says, "Yes, Detective, please have a seat and someone will be out for you."

I sit on a brown leatherette couch along a wall opposite the reception desk. A glass coffee table is in front of the couch. On the wall behind the couch are framed color portraits of the president of the United States and of the FBI director. A large corkboard on another wall holds posters of the Bureau's Ten Most Wanted Fugitives. The faces are all male, as unsmiling as the female lobby guard's. Their crimes include bank robbery, murder, racketeering, escape from prison, and terrorism. Thanks to Seal Team Six, Osama bin Laden is no longer on that list.

I select a magazine from among those on the coffee table. Slim pickings: *Federal Law Enforcement Journal, The Catalog of Tactical Weaponry, The Grapevine* (official publication of the Society of Former Special Agents of the FBI), *Crime Scene Technology* . . . It would be nice if they threw in an *Entertainment Weekly* or *People*, just to lighten the mood.

Before I can make a choice, a woman comes through the door from the inner offices. She is in her thirties, with shoulder-length auburn hair, green eyes, and freckles, and is wearing a navy-blue suit, white blouse, and low black leather heels. She doesn't have pigtails, but otherwise, she reminds me of the girl in the Wendy's hamburger chain logo. The model for the Wendy's girl is the daughter of the chain's founder, Dave Tomas; he named his restaurants after her. I'll admit to scarfing down a Dave's Double Stack from time to time, those times being whenever I pass one of the restaurants and haven't recently eaten.

Wendy offers her hand and says, "Detective Starkey, I'm Special Agent Sarah Caldwell." I wonder why FBI agents always think that they're special. As I rise and return her handshake, she says, "I'll show you to Agent Morrissey's office."

I follow her through the door and down a hallway, past offices whose doors are all closed, until we come to one whose door is open, and we go in. It is a large corner office, nicely appointed with furnishings several cuts above standard government issue.

A man stands from behind the desk and comes around to greet me. You call Central Casting and order up a poster FBI agent and you get Daniel Morrissey. He is tall, about six two or three, maybe one hundred ninety pounds, with black hair cut short, and wide shoulders. Morrissey is one of those fortunate guys who still look like they are thirty when they are into their forties and fifties, like Paul Newman did. He is wearing the same kind of suit as Agent Caldwell, but with pants instead of a skirt, and the addition of a red-and-blue striped tie: the standard-issue FBI uniform ever since the days of J. Edgar Hoover, who, I've heard, sometimes wore a dress and heels when off duty.

Detectives usually shrug off their suit coats and loosen their ties (if they ever tighten the knots at all, which I didn't) when working at their desks. Maybe that's against FBI regs. Morrissey has his suit coat on. Maybe he sleeps in his suit just in case he's called into action during the night.

"Dan Morrissey," he says as he shakes my hand. "It's a pleasure to meet you, Detective Starkey."

Morrissey is either a very nice guy, or a good liar, because the Feds always do their homework. I'll admit that I wasn't the easiest guy to work with, especially during my drinking days. I never let inconsequential things like rules or playing well with others stand in the way of closing a homicide investigation.

"Good to meet you too," I tell him.

We are mutually pleased to meet one another.

He returns to his desk chair, gesturing for me and Agent Caldwell to take the two wooden guest chairs in front of his desk.

For a trained investigator like myself, this is a revelatory moment. Rather than having all of us sit on the grouping of couch and club chairs over by the window, Morrissey put himself in the catbird seat, relegating Caldwell and me to positions of subservience. The idea is to make you feel like you're in the school principal's office to answer for some bad

behavior. The chairs seem lower than normal, so we are looking up at him. Maybe he had the chair legs sawed shorter.

Morrissey obviously wants visitors to know that, on his
turf, he is large and in charge. Also reinforcing this idea is
the fact that he doesn't ask if I want a beverage, let alone
a doughnut. That treatment is reserved for VIPs apparently.
Or maybe there'd been a federal budget cut and the snack
money is needed for bullets. But no problem. I learned in the
marines to do without the niceties of life, which sometimes
included food, water, and enough ammo, and still accomplish
the mission. Lock and load and bring it on.

"So, Detective Starkey," Morrissey begins, "you have a
distinguished record in the Marine Corps and with the Chicago Police Department."

Just as I thought. J. Edgar Morrissey had pulled my file.
I wonder if he knows about that Milky Way I pilfered from
Talbot's Pharmacy when I was six. No problem if he does
because the statute of limitations on petty theft has long since
run out.

"Better than some, worse than others," I reply in an
attempt at modesty, and also the god's honest truth.

"We'll be involved in your case if it's determined that the
murders of Lawrence Henderson and his wife are in some
way related to his position with the Manatee National Bank, a
federally insured institution," he informs me, something that
I already know.

Morrissey looks at Agent Caldwell for the first time. I
have good peripheral vision and have been checking her out
ever since we sat down and she crossed her legs, causing her
skirt to ride up on her tanned, muscular thighs. Brother Tim-
othy taught us that we cannot control our thoughts, only our
actions, and that is enough.

"If we do work together, Sarah will act as your liaison," Morrissey tells me, which more than makes up for the lack of doughnuts.

"That's fine," I say, smiling at Agent Caldwell. What you want most in a partner is competence, but nice legs don't hurt.

Morrissey continues: "Based on what I've learned from Chief Cullen, I'm calling in a forensic accounting team from Miami to audit the Manatee National Bank's books."

I wonder how Morrissey can already have obtained enough evidence to get a judge to issue a search warrant to allow the audit. What I have so far about a possible connection between the murders and Morrissey's bank is . . . nothing. Usually you have to say more to a judge than, "I really want a search warrant, Your Honor."

Then I realize that, in this post-911 world, the FBI can do just about anything it wants.

"That'll be very helpful," I tell him. There is nobody better than I am at stating the obvious.

Morrissey looks at his watch. "Unless you've got something else, why don't you and Agent Caldwell grab some lunch and get acquainted."

"Works for me," I tell him.

I volunteer to drive. Agent Caldwell follows me to my Vette, checks it out, gives a low whistle, and says, "Bitchin' ride, Detective."

"Thanks. Call me Jack."

"And I'm Sarah."

Progress is being made in our relationship.

I don't open her car door because that kind of chivalry is ancient history to modern women, especially those who are trained in armed and unarmed combat, and packing. Try to be a gentleman and you might get your ass handed to you.

Sarah strokes the leather upholstery. "This'd be a '63, I'd guess, with the 340 horsepower V8."

And this could be the start of a beautiful friendship, to paraphrase Rick in *Casablanca*. Maybe I should whistle "As Time Goes By."

As we pass through the guard gate, I ask her, "What do you drive?"

"For work, a government-issue black Suburban. For pleasure, a Porsche 911 and a Ducati 1200 Enduro."

Too cool for school. I might have to chat with Marisa about having an open relationship.

Just kidding.

I think.

I exit the parking lot, swing right onto West Gray Street and say, "Your town—where should we eat?"

"You like Cuban food?"

Not the time to tell her I'm dating a woman who can cook that cuisine well enough to make Fidel weep, so I just say, "Sure do."

"There's a place I like on West Columbus called La Terisita. *Arroz con pollo* to die for."

"Sounds good."

I also don't mention that the last time I was in a Cuban restaurant I almost did die. My daughter was meeting with one of the clients of her law firm in Miami about two years ago. I took her to Amador's Café Cubano on Lincoln Road in Miami Beach. During the meal, a man entered the café, approached a table where another man and a woman were dining, shot the man dead, and then shot himself. A love triangle gone bad. Do they ever not go bad?

Sarah directs me on surface streets to a two-story pink stucco building with a green awning. I turn into an adjoining gravel lot. Inside a young man wearing a white cotton shirt called a guayabera, calls out from behind the bar: "Hey, Sarah. Your usual table?"

"Hey, Mateo. That'll be good."

I follow her to a table at the back wall of the dining room. Good tradecraft: always have your back to the wall and a good view of the door. A waitress whose nameplate says she's Nell brings menus. I scan mine, then say, "Why don't you order for both of us?"

Nell returns after a few minutes. Without looking at her menu, Sarah orders a nice selection of Cuban food: *arroz con pollo, carne con papas, camarones fritos,* and *flan de queso* for dessert, accompanied by café Cubano.

The meal order reinforces my impression that there is, in fact, something special about Special Agent Sarah Caldwell. She is lovely, and, in addition to her career and her excellent choice of vehicles, she is a gourmand. Many women will tell a waiter, "I'll have a small salad with light vinaigrette on the side." To which the waiter will reply, "And for your entrée, madam?" And she will answer: "Oh, that *is* my entrée." Or she might ask another woman at the table if she'd like to split the salmon entrée with her. My reaction to that always is: Why bother to suit up and take the field if you're not going to play the game? People can eat whatever they want, but there are certain kinds of people I choose not to dine with.

"Bitchin' order," I comment.

"My last posting was the Miami field office. Another agent was from a Cuban family. He introduced me to the cuisine."

"And before Miami?"

"I'm from Minneapolis. I graduated from the University of Minnesota, then did a stint in the marines and went to the FBI Academy in Quantico."

A fellow marine. This was getting to be a serious test of my mutual understanding with my main squeeze.

"*Semper fi*," I say.

"You too?"

"Before you were born. We used mules to pull the artillery."

She laughs. "What are your marching orders for my case?" I ask her.

"To aid your investigation in any way I can. If it's determined that we have standing, of course. So let's see where the bank audit leads and go from there."

"Deal."

Our food arrives. It's delicious and there's a lot of it. Thankfully no active shooters interrupt us because I eat myself into a semi-stupor. I'm glad I already did my morning run along the beach. Staying awake during the drive home will be challenge enough.

8.

Shoe Leather

"So your FBI liaison's a babe," Cubby says when I walk into his office and drop onto the couch, putting the coffee and doughnut I picked up in the break room on the side table. Sometime during the drive from Tampa, the effect of the large lunch partially wore off, leaving just enough room for a light snack.

Cubby joins me in a club chair near the couch.

"I'm surprised straight-arrow Morrissey told you that," I say.

"He didn't. He just said you'd be working with Special Agent Sarah Caldwell. Her photo's on the FBI website."

"My interest in Agent Caldwell is purely professional, Cubby."

"So you won't mind if I share her photo with Marisa."

"Let's not bother her with shop talk."

"So next up is Manatee National Bank?"

I take a bite of doughnut. Strawberry jelly, my favorite. A dollop of jelly falls onto my shirtfront. An occupational hazard.

"After the doughnut, I mean," he adds. "And changing your shirt."

"I want to talk to the senior people at the bank, and after that to the Hendersons' family and friends. At some point, I want to go into the Henderson house and look around. Never know what you might find."

"I'll arrange for you to enter the house. Do you want help with the interviewing?"

"I'll do it myself."

Many cases are solved using confidential informants. But an ace investigator like me has to at least look busy interviewing people and poking around for clues until a snitch comes forward and tells me who did it.

After my meeting with Cubby, I drive to The Drunken Parrot to check in with Sam Long Tree. Sam is more than just my bartender. He is a friend I can trust to manage the bar while I'm off detecting. He doesn't need the bartender job. As a member of the Seminole tribe, which controls the casino business in Florida, he gets a share of the tribe's multibillion-dollar gambling revenue. When I asked him why he wants to be a bartender, he just shrugged and said, "It's good to stay busy." I guess when you are six foot six, a chiseled two hundred seventy pounds, and rich, you can do whatever the hell you want. He did tell me once that if I ever want to sell the bar, he'd be interested.

"Hi, boss," Sam says when I come into the bar through the back entrance.

I tell him about my assignment with the Fort Myers Beach PD. "I don't know how much time this case will take," I say.

"No problem. I'll take care of the bar. Just catch that stone-cold killer and make the world a better place."

9.

No Clue, Clock Radio, or Stadium Blanket

The Manatee National Bank is located in an eighteen-story glass tower on First Street in downtown Fort Myers, the tallest structure in the city, except for a new condo building just north of the bank on the Caloosahatchee River.

Fort Myers never developed into a major center of commerce in the way that other Florida coastal cities like Miami, Tampa, and Jacksonville did. Marisa said that's because the city has no deep-water shipping port and few major corporate employers. And there are not the kind of gulf-front beaches that attract resort hotels. Over the years, the city government and various business committees announced grand plans for a downtown revitalization, but they always petered out short of their goals. The bank building and a few other shorter office towers, a new marina, and a few riverfront condos are the greatest visible successes; for some urbanites, Starbucks finally opening a downtown store at the corner of Broadway and First Street was even more important.

The Boston Red Sox have a spring training stadium, City of Palms Park, in the city; it got old, there was not enough parking or other amenities, and the team threatened to move to Sarasota. Rather than lose the team, Lee County ponied up enough money for a new stadium, JetBlue Park, a miniature replica of Fenway Park. The Minnesota Twins hold spring training at Hammond Stadium in Fort Myers, which was recently remodeled.

I don't care about Starbucks, not a fan of their overpriced brown water with Italian names, but having two Major League spring training stadiums nearby, where I can scarf down hot dogs and see the teams close up, makes Fort Myers okay in my book, even though they are American League teams. The Cubs flirted with City of Naples a few years ago, but Mesa, Arizona, their spring training headquarters, finally agreed to build a replica of Wrigley Field for the team and they stayed put. Naples came *that* close to truly being paradise.

There are some nice residential neighborhoods in Fort Myers, but also some not-so-nice ones with a gang problem and a resultant high crime rate. Cubby Cullen was offered the Fort Myers police chief's job, with a substantial salary increase, a few years ago. He turned it down. He told me he'd rather issue citations to college kids for underage drinking, and chase boat thieves, than dodge gangbangers' gunfire. However, Cubby now has a major murder investigation on his hands. Violent crime has found him, even in his tranquil little town.

~

I TURN into the bank parking lot, locate a visitor's space, and enter the lobby. There is a Manatee retail banking office on the first floor. That's where I have my business and personal accounts. The executive offices are on eighteen. The rest of the building is filled with law, accounting, and investment firms, a commercial real estate brokerage office, and other companies that are successful enough to afford the high rent.

In my younger days, there were small community banks that knew you and felt an obligation to support the local economy. They sponsored Little League teams and contributed to local charities. People had checking and passbook savings accounts. You got the choice of a clock radio or stadium blanket when you opened an account, and if you wrote a check on insufficient funds, you got a phone call from your personal banker giving you the opportunity to make it good.

Then things changed. Banks grew and consolidated into giant financial service institutions whose main concerns are profit for the shareholders, high stock prices, and generous executive compensation packages. Individual customers are seen as a necessary nuisance served only to appease the regulators. When banks got into trouble for helping to create the subprime mortgage collapse, we—you and me—via our tax money, bailed them out.

Cubby set up meetings for me with three of the bank's top surviving officers: an executive vice president and two senior VPs. An officer in his department prepared background on each man for me. Cubby called the men and explained that I was the detective in charge of investigating the Henderson murders; he didn't add the fact that I was also investigating the bank, looking for any sign of illegal activity that could have gotten Lawrence Henderson and his wife killed. The FBI would position its audit as a routine check by bank examiners.

The elevator opens directly into the bank's executive offices. There is a reception desk manned by an attractive young woman. My first meeting is with the executive VP, Reynold Livingstone III. Guys with names like that don't work in the mail room, or wear name tags on their shirts. Livingstone and the two other men I'm seeing are all shareholders in Manatee Holdings, the privately held company that owns the bank. The late Lawrence Henderson was the majority shareholder.

The receptionist informs me that Mr. Livingstone is expecting me and leads me to his office. The background says he got his undergraduate degree from Yale and an MBA from Wharton. His grandfather, the first Reynold Livingstone, owned orange groves in Lee County, and the second RL had developed those into golf course communities and shopping malls. Fortunately for Reynold, his grandfather hadn't decided to attend the police academy.

In my previous life as a detective, before moving to Florida, I had a battered, government-issue metal desk facing my partner's desk in an open squad room with peeling grey paint on the walls, dirty windows that blocked the sunlight, and an acrid aroma of perspiration and burned coffee held in place by the substandard HVAC system that was probably installed by some pol's unlicensed nephew. There was constant background noise of buzzing fluorescent lights, ringing telephones, and loud conversations salted and peppered with curse words. Rather than describe Livingstone's office I'll just say, imagine the polar opposite of my old homicide squad room.

Livingstone comes from behind a desk the size of a Ping-Pong table and greets me with a smile and a firm handshake. He is in his forties, I guess. He has a deep tan, from golf, I imagine, not yard work. He wears the standard-issue bankers uniform: navy pin-striped suit, starched white shirt, blue tie with little crossed golf clubs on it, and black loafers. Not unlike the FBI uniform, but made of better fabrics. As we shake hands, I notice a monogram, RL III, on his right shirt cuff. "Hello, Detective Starkey," he says. "I'm Reynold Livingstone."

I guess that, when you have a Roman numeral after your name, it's considered pretentious to pronounce it, as in: "I'm Reynold Livingstone the Third." That would be like me saying, "I'm Jack Starkey the First."

RL III gestures toward two club chairs near the windows. When we're seated, he says, "I'll help your investigation in any way I can."

I begin with the obvious question: "Do you have any idea who'd want to kill Lawrence Henderson and his wife?"

"None at all. Larry was a terrific fellow. He had no enemies I ever knew about."

"Can you think of anyone who might be angry with the bank? Someone denied a loan, foreclosed upon, recommended a bad investment to, anything like that?"

"All of those things happen, so that's certainly a possibility. But no customer has ever expressed dissatisfaction deep enough to threaten murder, as far as I know."

He is silent for a moment, strokes his chin, then adds, "Actually, there *was* an incident involving a repossession of a commercial fishing boat a few years ago. The owner told his loan officer that they'd take the boat away over his dead body. Unfortunately, that's what happened. When the repo guy and a sheriff's deputy showed up at the marina, there was a gunfight and the boat owner was killed. His son told a newspaper reporter that our bank would come to regret killing his father. So there's that."

Note to self: if the bank decides to repossess *Phoenix*, let 'em have the tub.

"How did you come to work at the bank?" I ask him. Maybe he squandered his trust fund on fast cars and faster women and had to earn a paycheck, like the rest of us working stiffs.

"I knew Larry from our country club. We occasionally golfed together. I was managing my family's real estate development business. Eight years ago, there was a slowdown, so I put new development on hold and was looking for something else to do. I heard that Larry was seeking investors to start a bank. We talked about that, and I decided to be part of the group. He asked me to join the management team and I accepted. You can only play so much golf, you know."

"What did Mr. Henderson do before that?"

"He was president of a regional banking company, with no ownership."

I already knew that from Cubby's background report. I also knew that Henderson's father, Matthew, had owned a dry-cleaning store in Fort Myers, that his mother, Jeanette, was a homemaker, and that his older brother, Tom, worked as a supervisor for the Lee County Highway Department. Cubby's departmental researcher, a young woman working on her master's degree in library science at Florida Gulf Coast University, is that good.

So Larry was the only Henderson who wore a white collar to work. He'd been a star wide receiver for North Fort Myers High School and attended the University of South Florida on a full football scholarship. Considered too small for the pros, he'd entered the Sunshine State National Bank's training program and rose from assistant loan officer to president. A real Horatio Alger story.

"How is Manatee National doing these days?"

"Very well. We consistently perform at or near the top of our peer group."

"What will you do now that you've lost your president?"

"There's a board meeting in three days to figure that out. I don't want the job. I don't know about Bob or Henry. I expect we'll hire a search firm."

Maybe he thinks the extra pay isn't worth the added responsibility, or maybe he's decided to go back into real estate development now that the market is hot again. If it's true that RL III doesn't want the top job, I can probably cross him off my list of suspects, unless he had some other reason for committing the murders that isn't apparent. Maybe Henderson cheated him on a golf bet.

We continue the Q&A for another fifteen minutes. I get nothing useful, nor do I from the other two guys, Robert Kerr and Henry Allen. In fact, the answers of all three men are very similar. Rehearsed? Or the truth? No way to know at this point.

I leave the bank without a clue, clock radio, or stadium blanket. Sometimes in detective work, you come up dry. Maybe the audit will find evidence of drug-money laundering or the funding of terrorist groups. Or maybe, while I was at the bank, someone walked into the Fort Myers Beach Police Department and confessed.

10.

Solid Citizens, One and All

Next up on my interview list is Larry Henderson's brother, Tom. The funeral he and his wife, Liz, had to arrange for his brother and sister-in-law was only three days ago. I can't begin to imagine how difficult it was for him and Liz to go through that, with his brother's children, Nathan and Elise, now living with them. People need varying amounts of time to grieve, but I've never met anyone who didn't want to do whatever he or she could to help catch the person who murdered a loved one.

I arranged to meet Tom Henderson for lunch at Mary's Kitchen, a café I like on South Cleveland Avenue in Fort Myers. When I enter the café, I spot a man sitting alone in a booth. He is tanned and rugged-looking, like a man who works outside, and he is wearing a green work shirt. Every other customer is with someone, so that must be Tom Henderson. Additionally there is a name patch on his shirt that says "Tom." The ace detective at work.

He nods at me when we make eye contact and stands when I get to the booth. "Detective Starkey?"

"In person. I'm sorry for your loss."

As I slide into the booth, he says, "This is a difficult time for us, but I want to do anything I can to help you catch the bastard who killed my brother and his wife."

Arlene, a waitress I know, brings ice water, fills our coffee cups, and takes our order. It is meat loaf day, so I go for it. Tom orders a burger. Another food quirk I have: some people, when ordering at a restaurant, ask the waitress, "Can I have the meat loaf?" As if the waitress might say "No, you can't. I don't like your looks." Mostly I keep things like that to myself lest people think I'm odd.

As we wait for our food, I decide to get right to it: "Do you know of anyone who'd want to kill your brother and his wife?"

"Of course I've thought about that. As far as I know, Larry and Marion have no enemies. Had no enemies. Maybe it was a robbery. Or mistaken identity."

"It didn't appear that anything was taken from the boat. His wallet was there, with three hundred in cash and credit cards. He was wearing a gold Rolex. Her wallet also was there, with cash and credit cards, and some expensive jewelry was left behind. What about your brother's activities beyond the bank?"

"Larry liked to play golf, fish, and sail and he served on the boards of several charitable organizations. He was a solid citizen."

Larry Henderson didn't seem like a man who would launder money through his bank for a drug cartel or embezzle the bank's funds or be involved in any other nefarious activity. But I arrested many people during my career in Chicago who didn't seem like the type to commit the crimes they did: top corporate executives, a Boy Scout leader, two college professors, and an Episcopal priest, among others.

I ask Tom about Marion. He describes a loving wife and ideal mother with many friends who volunteered at the church the family attended and at their children's school. He told me that Marion had been serving as the president of an environmental group whose name he could not recall. He said they put up barriers around sea turtle nests during hatching season, erected osprey nests on top of poles, campaigned to save the mangroves and the manatees, things like that.

Both Hendersons certainly seemed to be solid citizens. Pillars of the community.

"I can't imagine that anyone had a reason to murder my brother and sister-in-law," Tom Henderson says as our food arrives.

But someone had, and it was my job to figure out who, and why.

11.

Mr. Livingstone, I Presume?

I'm preparing my usual breakfast aboard *Phoenix* when my cell phone rings. My ringtone this week is Buddy Guy doing "Damn Right, I've Got the Blues." Love the riffs on his Stratocaster. I insert a strawberry Pop-Tart into the toaster and answer. Joe already ate his tuna and is off somewhere sleeping. Even on a houseboat, cats have their secret places.

"Jack, it's Sarah Caldwell."

"You Feds start your workday early. Maybe you need a union."

"It's nine thirty. Reveille was three-and-a-half hours ago, marine. I'm on my way to Fort Myers. We fast-tracked the bank audit, working with their accounting firm without notifying anyone at Manatee National. The accounting firm resisted that at first, but a court order persuaded them to keep it confidential."

"And the audit found enough for you to be driving to the bank."

"Someone has been embezzling. Big bucks. Has to be an insider with access, I'd say. Just south of nine hundred thousand over the past three years."

"Wowzer. I'd say the bank's accounting firm deserves a good scolding for missing that."

"The partner in charge of the bank's account went to lunch when he heard an FBI audit team was coming—and he took his passport. We're looking for him now."

"Any idea who's involved at the bank?"

"Not yet. Meet me there in an hour. You interviewed their top execs . . ."

"I neglected to ask if anyone had his hand in the cookie jar."

"So this time we will. I told a secretary that we need to talk to them about irregularities revealed by an audit of the bank's financial statements."

"We don't know that the embezzling is connected to the murders."

"Right. If it was Henderson, and someone discovered it, you'd think they'd just drop a dime on him, not murder him and his wife. So probably not Henderson, if there's a connection."

"If it's someone else, and Henderson found out, he could have been killed to keep him from reporting it to the police," I add. "That seems unlikely. How could the killer know that Henderson hadn't already reported it?"

"But confronting the three top guys, and gauging their reaction, is a good place to start."

"Ten Four," I respond, a phrase I've only heard cops on TV use.

I arrive at the bank at ten thirty and wait for Sarah in the parking lot. She pulls in at ten forty, having made the drive from Tampa in record time. Maybe she used her lights and siren.

She pulls in beside me, gets out of her car and into mine, nearly sitting on my bag of Dunkin' Donuts I'd picked up on the way. I snatch them away at the last possible moment and wonder if she thinks I was trying to grab her ass. If so, she doesn't say anything about it or reach for her pepper spray.

We enter the bank building and ride the elevator to the top floor. Sarah IDs us to the receptionist. A moment later, a well-put-together woman in her late fifties or early sixties comes through a door leading to the inner offices. She is dressed in a tan linen suit. I notice the reflection of the overhead lights on a very large diamond wedding ring on her finger. Her grey hair is done up in a hairdo involving braids. Either she makes a very good salary at the bank, or she is the one who took the nine hundred thou.

She smiles and says, "Hello, I'm Dorothy Marcus. Agent Caldwell and Detective Starkey, I presume?"

I wonder if Dorothy knows she's making reference to the famous quotation of Henry Morton Stanley who, upon locating David Livingstone in Africa, famously greeted him by saying, "Dr. Livingstone, I presume?" Or maybe she is just confirming our identity and I should get my head back into the game.

Sarah assures Dorothy that we are in fact those people.

"I have Mr. Kerr and Mr. Allen waiting for you in the conference room," she tells us. "If you will please follow me."

"And Reynold Livingstone?" Sarah asks.

"He was called away on urgent business."

"When was that?" I ask her.

"I believe it was just after I told him that an FBI agent and detective were coming to the bank to speak with him and Mr. Kerr and Mr. Allen about an audit."

"Did he say what that urgent business was?" Sarah inquires.

Dorothy raises her perfectly manicured eyebrows and says, "Oh, he would not share something like that with me."

As if that was beyond obvious to anyone who understands corporate protocol.

Sarah gives me that cop-to-cop, something's-rotten-in-the-State-of-Denmark look.

"We'll need Mr. Livingstone's home address," I tell Dorothy.

She looks completely nonplussed, which is an old-timey way of saying she looks like she might soil her undies.

"I don't know," she finally answers.

"You don't know his home address?" Sarah asks her.

"It's not that. I don't know if I'm allowed to give it out without his permission."

"We'd rather not have to sweat it out of you down at the station," I say, in my best noir-detective voice.

"Or we could get a warrant," Sarah tells her. "We're investigating two murders. But time is of the essence. We need to move fast. Mr. Livingstone could be in danger."

Dorothy looks startled by the mention of the murders, if not by my noir detective.

"Let me call him first. Please wait here."

She goes through the door to the inner offices and reappears a few minutes later.

"Mrs. Livingstone says he is not at home and he didn't answer his cell phone. But Mrs. Livingstone said it is all right to give you their home address."

She hands Sarah a piece of bank notepaper with the address written on it.

"Now I'll show you to the conference room for Mr. Kerr and Mr. Allen," she says.

I look at Sarah, who nods, knowing what I'm about to say.

"Not necessary," I tell her. "Thanks for your assistance."

From the *Detecting for Dummies* handbook: when trying to sort out suspects, always go first for the one on the run.

On the way down in the elevator, I say to Sarah, "Perhaps Livingstone's urgent business is in Mexico."

"At the current exchange rate, nine hundred thousand dollars is sixteen million, two-hundred and seventy-two thousand pesos," she says. "That'll buy a lot of margaritas and tacos."

Proving that Special Agent Sarah Caldwell would be a formidable opponent in Trivial Pursuit.

12.

Hanging Around at Home

I follow Sarah's car to the front gate of a golf course community called Royal Palm Estates, located ten miles east of downtown Fort Myers. She'd entered RL III's address into her GPS. She shows the guard her badge and nods in my direction. The gate swings open.

Guards at gated communities don't wear sidearms, but help is a phone call away if a peasant mob bearing farm implements tries to storm the barricades, seeking revenge upon the upper one-percenters who are (allegedly) oppressing them. In Naples, I never heard anyone say, "Let them eat cake." But you could get that impression from the lavish lifestyle on display. Not visible is the high level of charitable giving and other good works, but optics are everything.

We roll past Spanish- and Italianate-style mini mansions. Sarah parks in front of a two-story, tan-stucco house with a red tile roof and four-car garage. A Fort Myers PD cruiser, a brown Crown Vic, and a Royal Palm Estates security force SUV are parked in the driveway. That kind of vehicular lineup usually means something is amiss, or that free doughnuts are on offer.

Sarah and I get out of our cars and walk toward the house. A uniformed officer is standing beside the cruiser, chatting with the security guy. We show the officer our badges and he says, "They're in the garage."

The garage doors are open. I see three cars inside: a white Mercedes SUV, a black Porsche turbo convertible, and a powder-blue Bentley sedan. A golf cart occupies the fourth space. A man in a brown suit is standing beside the Bentley. The suit matches the Crown Vic, so that must be the Fort Myers detective. He is an African American man in his fifties, wearing Ray-Ban Aviator sunglasses. He has a powerful build, bald head, and a diamond stud in his left earlobe.

Sarah shows her badge and says, "I'm Special Agent Caldwell and this is Detective Starkey from Fort Myers Beach."

He looks at her, then me, and says, "Detective Don Morgan. Why are you here?"

"Mr. Livingstone is part of an ongoing investigation," Sarah tells him. "We're here to speak with him. Is he here?"

"It'll be a one-way conversation," Morgan says. "He's dead."

"The cause of death?" Sarah asks.

I'm letting her take the lead. The FBI has more clout in a situation like this than a dollar-a-year detective out of his jurisdiction.

"We're waiting for the crime scene people and the coroner," Morgan tells her. He explains that his wife found him hanging from a rafter with a rope around his neck and a footstool tipped over on the floor. He's still like that, we can see now, dangling beside the Mercedes SUV. I'm a car guy so I notice, even with a corpse hanging there, that it's a Mercedes GL550 AMG model. Premium ride. A senior bank exec could afford the car, even without stealing. But for some people, enough is never enough.

"Mind if we take a look?" I ask Morgan.

"Just don't touch anything," he answers.

Which is something of an insult, as if an FBI agent and a veteran detective would contaminate a crime scene.

Reynold Livingstone the Last (the background said that the couple have two daughters, but no sons).

I've been to the autopsies of people who died that way. They were all ruled suicides, except for one man who was a homicide. In that case, a typed suicide note matched to the victim's printer contained many grammatical errors such as, "I ain't got no more reason to live." The victim had graduated with honors in English lit from Northwestern. His wife's boyfriend was a carpenter, hired to remodel the couple's kitchen, who had dropped out of high school. As my father used to say, "If someone is merely misinformed, you can work with that person, but there ain't no workin' with stupid."

The widow and the carpenter are probably still making license plates for the State of Illinois.

After we have a good look, I say to Morgan, "You said his wife discovered the body?"

"Mrs. Livingstone, who is inside with one of our officers, called 911 and said there was a medical emergency at her house involving her husband," Morgan says. "When our uniform arrived, he found Livingstone hanging from the rope."

"Okay if we go inside and talk to Mrs. Livingstone?" Sarah asks him.

"First tell me more about why the FBI and Fort Myers Beach police are interested in her hubby," Morgan says.

Sarah does because it's Morgan's crime scene. Of course he'd heard about the Henderson murders, but not about the embezzlement.

"So I got the suicide and you got the alleged embezzlement and any other bank stuff," Morgan tells us.

"Right," Sarah assures him.

"Good to go then," he says.

An EMS van pulls up as we enter the house through a door from the garage. An attractive middle-aged woman with shoulder-length blonde hair, wearing a pink tee shirt and black yoga pants, is seated on a living room couch, with a female police officer in a chair beside her. The woman's eyes are red and she has a stricken look on her face. Mrs. Livingstone, I presume.

"I'm Special Agent Caldwell and this is Detective Starkey," Sarah says to both of them. She looks at the woman. "I'm sorry about your loss, Mrs. Livingstone. Do you mind if I ask you a few questions?"

"She hasn't given us a statement yet," the officer says, a bit testily. Her nameplate says "Ramirez."

"Detective Morgan said it'd be all right," I tell her.

She spreads her hands.

"In that case, be my guest."

"Do you know of any reason why your husband would want to take his life?" Sarah asks.

Her eyes tear up.

"No. We were very happy."

"How did you discover the body?" I ask her.

"I was on the treadmill, listening to an audiobook through headphones. It was 'All the Light We Cannot See' by Anthony Doerr. When I finished my workout I went into the kitchen and saw Ray's car parked in the driveway. Which was odd because he didn't tell me he was coming home. I looked for him in the house and then went into the garage . . ."

She began sobbing.

"Thank you," Sarah says. "We might have more questions for you later."

Sarah nods at Officer Ramirez and we go back into the garage. I thank Morgan for his cooperation and tell him that, if he wants to hear some good music, jazz and blues, he should stop in at The Drunken Parrot in Fort Myers Beach.

"Just might do that," he says.

"Discount for cops," I tell him.

He winks and says, "You're on."

Three days later, Sarah calls me while I'm at the bar to say that an examination of Livingstone's bank and brokerage accounts shows that he was nearly broke until large deposits began appearing about a year ago, adding up to the amount embezzled from his bank. A call from Detective Morgan told her why: Livingstone had a gambling problem, according to his wife, visiting Las Vegas often as well as the Arrowhead Casino in Immokalee, an agricultural town an hour's drive southeast of Fort Myers.

"Livingstone was the head of the bank's audit committee," Sarah reports, "so it was easy for him to cover up his crime."

"So it's possible Larry Henderson found out about the embezzling, confronted Livingstone, and, before he could report it, Livingstone hired a hit man, given that it's unlikely he would do the wet work himself," I say.

"A possibility. The FDIC doesn't reimburse a bank for theft, so we're out of it," Sarah says. "The murder investigation is all yours, Jack. Good luck with that."

On my boat, I change into my workout clothes and do a long run on the beach. I do my best thinking while running. One thing I immediately decide is that I will never let myself look like the porcine old guy I pass who is wearing little black bikini swim trunks, a style adopted mainly by European tourists. Guy like that should wear a muumuu.

My next decision, after admiring a number of young ladies strolling the beach who look much better in their bikinis, is to see if I can somehow determine if Larry Henderson actually had discovered Livingstone's embezzlement. If he did, maybe he told Robert Kerr and Henry Allen, the two Manatee National Bank senior VPs. It would be interesting to see how they held up under my enhanced interrogation technique, which would consist of me eating doughnuts in front of them and not offering them any.

13.

Citizens for a Sane Environment

Before my morning run, I need to catch up on my editing of *Stoney's Dilemma*. I am interested in how the other Jack is handling the Lonnie Williams interview. In order to keep up with other fictional crime solvers such as John D. MacDonald's Travis McGee, John Sandford's Lucas Davenport, James Lee Burke's Dave Robicheaux, Michael Connelly's Harry Bosch, and Chris Knopf's Sam Acquillo, Bill had to make Jack Stoney better than me. Poetic license is what they call it. I don't mind. Who would want to have all of his weaknesses and mistakes revealed to millions of readers? Not this particular cowboy. So, Stoney, let's see you in action.

Stoney wrote out his promise of a deal with Lonnie Williams, the scumbag who'd kidnapped, raped, and murdered young Christine Petrocelli, on the yellow legal pad. He invented meaningless legalese, with a lot of "whereases," "party of the first part and party of the second part," a "let it be known by this presence," and references to nonexistent case law. He signed the gobbledygook, slid the notepad across the table to Williams, and said, "Can you read this, Lonnie, or do I need to read it to you?"

Williams studied the document carefully, moving his lips as he read, or pretended to read, then said, "Looks okay."

Stoney slid the pen to Williams.

"Your turn. Write down exactly what you did to Christine Petrocelli."

It took Williams twenty minutes and three pages to document his crime, in part because he was printing. He must have missed the class when they taught cursive in school, Stoney reflected. At least he didn't dot his i's with smiley faces.

When Williams finished, Stoney said, "Now put your John Hancock at the bottom."

Williams furrowed his brow. "John who?"

So he'd missed history along with cursive writing, Stoney thought. "Never mind. Sign your name. Use an X if you can't spell it."

Williams printed his name. Stoney took the pad and scanned what Williams had written. Then he pushed back his chair, stood up, and told Lonnie Williams that he was being arrested for kidnapping, rape, and murder.

"Hey, what about my fuckin' deal?" Williams asked.

"Long story short," Stoney said. "You're fucked."

He took the paper he'd written the deal on, ripped it into small pieces, and let them fall onto the tabletop like confetti.

I had no edits on that part. It was just the way I'd dealt with a perp named Paulie Gianello. Normally I am not that loose with a suspect's constitutional rights. But you harm a child and all bets are off.

I just finished my morning run and am walking down the dock toward my houseboat when I notice Cubby Cullen's Explorer pulling into the Salty Sam's parking lot. Cubby gets out and walks toward me. I would go to meet him halfway, but I did an extra two miles and have just enough energy left to make it to the *Phoenix*. Aging takes a toll.

"Something's happened, Jack," he says as we walk toward my houseboat. "A man was found dead in his fishing boat off Sanibel early this morning. Shot in the head."

"Who was he?"

"A guy named Russell Tolliver. Owns four car dealerships in Lee County and serves as a state legislator representing this district."

"Anything about the bullet yet?"

"Not till the autopsy. I saw the body. A .22 hollow-point fragments upon impact, making it hard to match. No shell casing, no fingerprints, just like with the Hendersons."

We reach the *Phoenix*, step aboard, and go into the galley. I flip on the coffee machine. Marisa has an expensive Nespresso model that makes perfect whatchamacallit drinks, but the controls on fancy machines like that are far too complicated for me. I might as well try to fly a 747.

"Two execution-style murder incidents in boats in the same area within a short time of one another," I say as the coffee begins to brew. "I'd say they're related."

"That's why I'm asking you to take on the Tolliver murder too," Cubby tells me.

"In for a penny, in for a pound, Cubby."

"I appreciate it, Jack. I gotta get to the station. I'll let you know when I get the autopsy report, and we'll run background on Tolliver. We figure out the connection between him and the Hendersons, and we're halfway there."

Cubby departs. I pour a cup of coffee, thinking: halfway there, by maybe identifying the killer. The other half is catching him and getting proof he's the one. That half is always the hardest.

After I teamed up for a day with the CSIs at the Tolliver crime scene while it was still fresh, I planned to spend the rest of the week interviewing a list of Lawrence and Marion Henderson's friends and relatives, and a few more bank employees. I'd go back to the Tolliver murder after that.

I find out that everyone liked and admired the Hendersons and had no idea about who would have wanted them dead.

Marion Henderson's friends said her main extracurricular activity was serving as president of a group called Citizens For a Sane Environment. Apparently sanity means working against the forces of evil who would irreparably damage Florida's environment if left unchecked, Marion's sister, Lucy, told me. According to the group's website, one of its main initiatives is opposing a bill currently before the state legislature that would allow oil and natural gas drilling just fifty miles off the Florida Gulf Coast, superseding a current law prohibiting the drilling no closer than one hundred twenty-five miles, and in some areas, two hundred thirty-five miles.

Lucy, who is also a member of the group, told me that Democratic Representative Russell Tolliver was leading the opposition to the drilling bill in the legislature.

By the end of the week, I had the autopsy report on Russell Tolliver. Sure enough, he'd been shot in the head by a .22-caliber pistol, just like the Hendersons.

Interesting. Marion Henderson and Russell Tolliver both were opposing the drilling bill, and both, along with Marion's husband, who maybe was collateral damage, appear to have been murdered by the same person.

14.

Big Oil

I have an appointment with Lance Porter, the late Russell Tolliver's executive assistant. I wonder what Mr. and Mrs. Porter were thinking when they named their baby boy Lance. Maybe that the taunting of other children on the playground would toughen him up. I want to ask him details about Representative Tolliver's oil- and natural-gas-drilling bill opposition and about the bill's sponsors and other supporters.

Porter lives in Tallahassee, the state capital, but he's in Fort Myers to help his boss's family deal with their unexpected loss. The Tollivers have a house on McGregor Boulevard, near the Edison and Ford Winter Estates, where visitors can see the winter homes of Thomas Alva Edison and his pal, Henry Ford, and tour Edison's workshop, along with a museum and botanical garden.

Two days after Tolliver's murder, I drive to his house, where Porter said I should meet him. The funeral is the following day. He told me he had some time in the morning to speak with me. He said that his boss often fished the Pine Island Sound waters, sometimes alone and sometimes with friends.

I pull into the driveway of a brick Tudor on a large lot containing palm and oak trees and surrounded by a redbrick wall with a black iron gate that is open. I park, go onto the front porch, and ring the doorbell. After a moment, the door is opened by a man who says, "Detective Starkey? I'm Ross Tolliver, Russell's son."

Ross Tolliver is in his late twenties, I'd guess, of medium height, slim, with jet-black hair over his ears, green eyes, perfect white teeth, and a straight nose, giving him the look of a male model. He is wearing a white V-neck tennis sweater, its sleeves pushed up on his forearms, white flannel slacks, and tan suede loafers, no socks. He looks to have a fifty-dollar haircut. I pay twelve-fifty for mine at Buddy's, one of those old-fashioned barber shops with *Sports Illustrated* and fishing and hunting magazines in the rack, many of them several years old.

I wonder how Ross knew I was a detective rather than the pool man or a Jehovah's Witness canvassing the neighborhood. I suppose that no one but me was expected at ten A.M. I recall a joke I heard one night at the Baby Doll bar: Two Jehovah's Witnesses are canvassing a neighborhood. They walk onto a porch of one of the houses and one rings a doorbell. A man answers, invites the two in, seats them on the sofa in the living room, takes a chair, and says, "What it is you fellows have in mind?" One of the men thinks for a moment, looks at his partner, then says, "I really don't know, sir. We've never gotten this far before."

I introduce myself, and Ross holds the door open for me to enter. "Thank you for trying to find my father's murderer," he says. "My mother thanks you too. She's upstairs sleeping. She's taking a medication her doctor prescribed. Are you making any progress with your investigation?"

Law enforcement officials always tell the news media that they are not able to discuss the details of an "active investigation." Which often means they haven't a clue. But families deserve to know more than that.

"It's still early," I answer, "but I do have some promising leads. Please tell your mother that I will do all that I can to find the person responsible for your father's death."

He asks no more about that and says, "Lance is out back, by the pool. I'll show you the way."

I think about telling him that any detective worth his weight in Pop-Tarts could find the pool on his own, it was likely to be somewhere in the vicinity of the backyard, but that would be rude, so I follow him through the house and out a back door to the rear patio.

Lance Porter is seated at a round wrought-iron table under a large green-and-white striped canvas umbrella, near a large swimming pool. He's talking on a cell phone. Ross goes back into the house. Porter looks at me and holds up his index finger in a just-a-moment gesture. He ends the call, stands, offers his hand, and says, "Detective Starkey, I'm Lance Porter. Have a seat. Do you want coffee?" He has a large ceramic mug in front of him.

Porter has the muscular build of a man who might have been an athlete in his school days, and who has kept in shape. Or maybe a military man who did more than push papers during his tour of duty. His firm handshake adds to this impression.

"Thanks, but I'm all coffee-ed out," I say. Without doughnuts, what's the point? Fries without ketchup. Penn without Teller. A state fair without . . . all the stuff they have at state fairs.

When we're seated, he reaches for a leather briefcase on one of the other chairs, opens it from the top, pulls out a manila folder, and puts it in front of me.

"This is a copy of the oil and gas drilling bill you asked about," he explains. "House Resolution 0022. So you think that Russell's opposition to this bill might have had something to do with his murder?"

"It's a possibility," I answer. "Just one of several I'm looking at. Tell me about the sponsors and main supporters of the bill."

Of course I'm not looking at any other possibilities, but he doesn't need to know that.

"A Republican by the name of Arthur Wainwright, who represents a Palm Beach County district, is the primary sponsor of the House bill. As you might imagine, the oil and gas industry, via its lobbyists, vigorously supports the measure."

"In addition to Russell Toliver, were there any other vocal opponents of the bill?"

"Every Democrat in the House and Senate is automatically opposed to all Republican legislation. And vice versa. That's why nothing ever gets done in government, except for the occasional bipartisan bill for something like funding the state mosquito control program."

Just then a mosquito lands on his neck. He swats it, leaving a tiny blood smear. Maybe it's time to increase the mosquito program's funding.

"Did Russell know Lawrence or Marion Henderson?" I ask him.

"That was such a tragedy. Russell knew them both very well. I met them just once at a fund-raiser. They were generous contributors to Russell's campaigns, even though they were Republicans, and Marion's organization, Citizens for a Sane Environment, also strongly opposed the drilling bill. In fact, it was Marion who enlisted Russell's support for defeating the bill."

"Was the bill going to pass?"

"Do you know much about state politics?"

"I'm from Illinois, where four of the last seven governors went to prison and two of them are currently incarcerated."

He laughs.

"It's not quite *that* bad in Florida. But here, like everywhere else, money rules. Individual donors to political campaigns want favors, and get them, and lobbyists actually write some of the bills."

"So some lobbyist wrote the drilling bill?"

"Yes. It was drafted by a group called The American Energy Independence Coalition, headquartered in Washington. Aka Big Oil. They've got a megabuck war chest funded by the oil and gas companies."

"Megabuck" gets my detective's juices flowing. Love and money: the two leading causes of murder. Now there is money to follow.

"So to answer your question," Porter says, "it looked like the drilling bill was a slam dunk until Marion Henderson's group started to organize opposition to it, and enlisted Russell's support. The head count of votes still favors passage by a good margin, but I'm sure the sponsors didn't like Marion and Russell stirring things up by highlighting possible environmental problems from the drilling."

"Did Russell ever receive a death threat?"

"Yes, more than once. Comes with the job. I always turned them over to the Capitol Police. None were ever credible. Just cranks."

"It's rare that a killer makes a threat first," I tell him. "But it does happen, so it's good to run them all down."

I thank Porter for his help, consider offering my condolences for his name as well as for the death of his boss, think better of it, and show myself out, having learned the route on the way in without having to leave a trail of bread crumbs.

During my drive back to Fort Myers Beach, I call the Florida Capitol Police headquarters in Tallahassee, tell the woman who answers who I am and what I need, and am transferred to Sgt. Jim Mikanopy (I had the woman spell his last name) in the Protective Operation Section.

The name is familiar. Sam Long Tree gave me a book about the history of the Seminole Nation. During the 1800s, there was a famous chief with that name. When the sergeant comes on the line, I ask him if he knows Sam.

"I do," Mikanopy says. "He's the vice chairman of the Seminole Tribe of Florida's Tribal Council. I'm the chairman."

"Sam and I work together."

"Thanks to our casinos, Sam doesn't have to work, and neither do I," the sergeant says. "But it gets boring sitting around cashing checks. Now how can I help you, Detective?"

"You know about the murder of Rep. Russell Tolliver, I assume."

"Of course."

"I'm leading that investigation, along with the possibly related murders of the Hendersons of Fort Myers."

"A tragedy," Mikanopy says. "Who does something like that?"

"That's what I'm trying to find out. Lance Porter told me you've investigated a number of death threats to Russell Tolliver. He said none were credible."

"That's right. We've developed a profile as a way of assessing whether the person making the threat meets certain criteria to be taken seriously. No system's perfect, but ours has worked so far."

"Was there a recent threat that mentioned Tolliver's opposition to the bill relating to oil and gas drilling in the gulf?"

"No, nothing like that."

I thank him for his time.

I decide that I need to find out more about Rep. Arthur Wainwright and his pals at the American Energy Independence Coalition. Maybe if I show up in their offices and flash my badge, they'll confess, if not to the three murders, then to whatever else it is they're doing wrong at the moment. There's always something.

But they probably will not confess, so some good old-fashioned detective work is called for, and I am nothing if not old-fashioned.

15.

Deepwater Horizon

Marisa cooks one of her wonderful Cuban feasts for us at her house. As always, she wraps up some leftovers for Joe. Tonight he gets sea bass without the yellow rice and plantains, which she knows he doesn't like.

I usually don't remember my dreams, but the next morning I do: it involved the catastrophic explosion of BP's Deepwater Horizon oil drilling platform in 2010, which caused eleven deaths and a massive oil spill in the Gulf of Mexico off the Louisiana coast. No surprise, I'd just seen the movie.

In my dream, I was on the rig as the character played by Mark Wahlberg when the explosion happened. Obviously that's the kind of natural disaster Marion Henderson's group, Citizens For a Sane Environment, is seeking to at least minimize by preventing the drilling boundary from moving in to fifty miles.

So the question of the moment remains: Was it their opposition that got the Hendersons and Tolliver killed? Is there some faction of the Big Oil industry that nefarious? Does the American Industry Independence Coalition have a hit man on the payroll?

Pondering all that during my morning beach run, I decide that I need to talk to Rep. Arthur Wainwright. The Florida State Legislature is in session, but when I call his office, his admin assistant tells me he's at home in Palm Beach. Not surprising because, in Florida, being a state legislator is not a full-time job. So it will be off to Palm Beach for me.

Back at my houseboat, I shower, power up my laptop and Google Wainwright's name. I click on a link to his website. His photo is on the home page. He's seated behind a desk, his hands folded, with US and State of Florida flags on staffs behind him. He is a patrician-looking fellow in his fifties, with a full mane of silver hair, an aquiline nose, and a cleft chin.

I click on a tab marked "résumé." The man has impressive credentials—that is, if he hasn't made them up, as some people do. It's amazing how many Navy SEALs, Harvard graduates, Purple Heart recipients, karate black belts, and Eagle Scouts are out there, if résumés are to be believed.

It was my boyhood dream to be a starting pitcher for the Cubs. I got as far as American Legion ball when I hurt my arm and my dad couldn't see the point of paying for Tommy John surgery to keep my baseball career going. Maybe I should pad my curriculum vitae to say I was a Cy Young Award winner for the Cubs before becoming a Chicago cop.

If Wainwright's résumé is accurate, he graduated from Harvard and then from Yale Law School, served as a naval officer, and is CEO of Wainwright Industries, a company started by his father that owns orange groves, builds custom homes, manufactures medical devices, and operates a chain of urgent care centers.

I'm about to dial the home number the assistant gave me when my phone rings. The caller ID says it's Claire, my ex-wife.

I met Claire when I was a rookie patrolman and chased down a perp who'd grabbed her purse while she was walking in Old Town. We had a great marriage until I screwed it up by trying to deal with the stress of the job by stopping off at the Baby Doll Polka Lounge on the way home to tell my troubles to a pal named Jack Daniels.

The drinking made me "emotionally unavailable" to her and to our daughter, Jenny, Claire said. No question that she was right. After our divorce, she got an MBA from Northwestern. She's a senior vice president with a bank and has been dating an orthopedic surgeon, a big step up from an alcoholic homicide detective.

Obviously, "dating" is too mild a term.

When I answer the phone, Claire says, "Jack, I'm calling so that you won't be surprised when the invitation arrives in the mail."

"Okay," I say. "What am I being invited to?"

"To my wedding."

16.

The Island

I take I-75 south and east across the southern tip of Florida. The stretch of the highway that runs through the Everglades is called Alligator Alley because many of the reptiles can be seen sunning themselves along the banks of drainage ditches paralleling the road. Accidents happen when drivers are scanning the ditches to see the prehistoric creatures.

I merge from Alligator Alley onto I-595 east, connect to I-95 north, exit onto South Dixie Highway north, leading into West Palm Beach, and then turn onto a bridge connecting the mainland to the island of Palm Beach.

There is no guard gate to prevent the hoi polloi from crossing onto the treasured island, but sometimes a Palm Beach police cruiser is waiting to follow any car that looks suspicious, meaning any vehicle costing less than the gross national product of Luxembourg. I wave at the young officer in the cruiser. He doesn't wave back or follow me. I guess a classic Corvette passes muster.

Locals call Palm Beach "The Island" in the way that New Yorkers call their berg "The City," as if you're supposed to know what they mean. As far as they're concerned, all the right sort of people do.

More than ten thousand Palm Beach residents occupy ten square miles of some of the most prime real estate in the nation. Funny thing is, you rarely see them. The shoppers on Worth Avenue, which I think of as Net Worth Avenue, are mainly tourists; Palm Beachers have personal shoppers. When you drive through the neighborhoods, with or without a police tail, you only see landscape crews perpetually manicuring the lush lawns and gardens, as well as delivery trucks and city utility crews.

For many, if not most, Palm Beach homeowners, those multi-multimillion-dollar estates are second, third, or fourth homes, rarely occupied, and then only during The Season—winter, to the rest of us. I've been there then, and still saw very few homeowners in the neighborhoods. Maybe they have helipads on the roofs. You can find them in the private clubs and fancy restaurants, but I wouldn't be admitted to the former and can't afford the latter. Actually I can afford to eat in those restaurants, but I don't want to pay exorbitant prices for small portions.

I make my way to South Ocean Drive, which runs north and south along the Atlantic coast. The houses are fenced, gated, and hotel-sized. "Behind every great fortune there is a crime," Balzac wrote. I remember that quotation from a college class in comparative literature. It's a clever phrase and was perhaps true in post-Napoleonic France. But, here on South Ocean Boulevard, I get the feeling that I've been transported back to that time and place. Can someone really earn all the wealth that these estates represent, by honest means? Of course they can, but not me, or anyone I know.

The wind is up, creating whitecaps on the Atlantic. A few surfers are riding boards on cresting waves, ignoring the possibility that they could become lunch for a great white shark (that has happened in recent years along this stretch of coastline).

The GPS on my cell phone directs me to a large, two-story, yellow-stucco palazzo with a green slate roof and a six-car garage. A large wrought iron gate swings open as I approach it. I notice a security camera mounted on a tall metal post. I drive through the gate, onto a circular driveway, and park near the front door of the house.

The door opens as I'm getting out of my car. A Man Mountain, in his thirties, with a bald head, wearing a well-tailored black suit and a don't-fuck-with-me expression, greets me by asking, "Are you Detective Starkey?"

I think about saying, "No, I'm a Jehovah's Witness," but I figure he isn't in the mood to hear that joke, is armed, and might be ordered to shoot unwelcome visitors on sight, so I tell him that I am the man he named.

"Are you carrying a weapon?" he asks.

"It's in my car."

He pats me down anyway. If he's pleased to not find any guns, or knives, or hypodermic needles, or that I'm not wearing a suicide vest under my white polo shirt with The Drunken Parrot logo, he doesn't show it.

"Mr. Wainwright is out by the pool," he says, giving his name as Alexi. "Follow me."

Just like Lance Porter. I guess that self-styled VIPs always wait for their guests out by the pool. I follow him through the foyer, living room, and kitchen to a sliding glass door leading to the backyard. The inside of the house is all antique furniture, marble floors, oriental rugs, and oil paintings hung in elaborate wooden frames on the walls. The kitchen is professional grade. I bet that Arthur Wainwright doesn't make his own meat loaf.

Man Mountain slides the door open and remains inside as I walk onto a back patio with a marble floor and lawn furniture, an outdoor kitchen with a gas grill, a sink, a refrigerator, and a round, wrought-iron dining table and chairs. Just beyond the patio is a swimming pool large enough to host Olympic races.

A man wearing a white bathrobe rises from a lounge chair beside the pool. He looks just like the photo of Arthur Wainwright from his website, but about ten to fifteen years older. Ah, vanity, thy name is Arthur.

He smiles warmly, offers his hand, and says, "Detective Starkey, I'm Art Wainwright. Let's have a drink and you can tell me how I can help you with your investigation."

We take seats at a round white wooden poolside table under a blue-and-white striped umbrella. A heavyset middle-aged Hispanic woman wearing a crisp white-and-grey maid's uniform appears beside us. I hadn't seen her come out of the house. Maybe she is permanently posted behind one of the nearby Calusa hedges, awaiting a signal from her boss that he needs something.

Art looks at his gold Rolex, says, "It's cocktail hour somewhere" (it's 11 A.M., so they're pulling out the wine corks in Rome), tells the maid he'll have a mimosa, and asks me what I'd like.

I assume the Wainwright household doesn't stock Berghoff Root Beer, so I ask for a Diet Coke. My host raises his eyebrows and says, "Well, Detective, whatever floats your boat." Not original, but I get the point. He is a player, and I'm not. The interview has not yet begun, and I'm already behind on points.

As the maid walks toward the house, Artie boy says, "You told my assistant in Tallahassee that you're looking into the deaths of Russell Tolliver and that couple from Fort Myers . . ."

"Lawrence and Marion Henderson."

"Well, Detective, I'm afraid that, after your long drive, I can't shed any light on that. Russ was a good man and I was shocked by his death. I've never heard of those other people."

I notice that he is avoiding using the word "murder." In my experience as a homicide detective, that either means something, or not. If detecting was easy, everyone could do it.

"I'm talking to people who knew the victims to see if there's a connection between them," I tell him.

He spreads his hands and says, "As I told you, I knew Russ, but not, uh . . ."

"Lawrence and Marion Henderson."

"Yes, them."

I'm finding his supposed inability to remember the names of two of the murder victims to be annoying, to the point where I'd like to punch him in his aquiline nose. But that might end the interview, so instead I ask, "Do you know any reason why someone would want to harm Mr. Tolliver?"

He leans back in his chair and looks at the sky, as if the answer is up there somewhere among the fluffy white clouds, then says, "Absolutely not." He shrugs, spreads his hands, and adds, "He owned car dealerships, you know. Maybe a dissatisfied customer?"

When I was an unmarried patrolman, I bought a used Chevy Caprice that threw a rod as I was driving it home. The salesman and the owner of the dealership were reluctant to do anything about that. I didn't consider killing them, that would have generated a lot of paperwork, so I mentioned my cousin, who worked for the city department in charge of licensing car lots. That did the trick.

Just as the maid arrives with our drinks, the door to the house slides open. A tall young woman with short blonde hair, wearing a robe similar to Art's, barefoot, comes out and walks toward us.

Without standing, Art says, "Detective Starkey, this is my wife, Jennifer."

Granddaughter is more like it. Always the gentleman, I stand and say, "I'm pleased to meet you, Mrs. Wainwright."

"Likewise, I'm sure," she says as she shrugs off her robe and drapes it over one of the chairs. She's wearing a black, two-piece bikini the width of dental floss. Killer bod. She stands on the edge of the pool, dives in, and begins swimming laps with a front crawl worthy of Michael Phelps.

"Jennifer was an All-America swimmer at the University of Florida in Gainesville," Art tells me. "I was the commencement speaker one year, and she was my student guide."

When I was working a serial-killer case in Naples, a town as wealthy as Palm Beach, but lower-key, I observed quite a few of these May-December relationships. The May was always young and pretty and the December was always old and rich. Whatever floats your boat.

After being distracted by Miss May, it's time to get to the point of my visit: "I understand you're sponsoring a piece of legislation in the House relating to offshore oil and gas drilling in the gulf, and that Mr. Tolliver was opposing the bill."

He sips his mimosa, wipes his mouth with the back of his hand, and says, "That's correct. But, while it's true that partisan politics have gotten quite nasty in recent years, we haven't resorted to hiring a hit man to eliminate the opposition." He smiles and adds, "At least not yet."

Interesting. I hadn't mentioned a hit man. Maybe that was significant, maybe it wasn't. Obviously detective work is not an exact science. More of a coin toss, sometimes. It doesn't seem like Art is going to confess, and thus lose this house, whatever cars are in that garage, his household staff, and, of course, his child bride.

He checks his Rolex again and tells me, "Unless there's something more I can help you with (as if he'd helped me) I need to get dressed for a lunch appointment."

Jennifer finishes her laps, climbs the ladder out of the pool, and slips on her robe.

"Jennifer will show you out," Art tells me.

I could find my own way, but I recalled that she'd guided Art around the UF campus, with an interesting result.

"I'd appreciate that," I say.

Impure thoughts appear unbidden along the way.

17.

Capital Crimes

The next morning, I face one of those difficult choices life presents from time to time: Pancakes, or a Belgian waffle?

Cubby and I are having breakfast at Stan's Diner so I can update him on my investigation. I go for the pancakes and he orders the waffle. The pancakes at Stan's are thick, big as a Frisbee, and chock-full of blueberries. The waffle comes with pecans and has those little square indentations that hold butter and warm maple syrup so well.

I tell Cubby about Marion Henderson's group, Citizens for a Sane Environment, about the oil and gas drilling bill, and the American Energy Independence Coalition. I cover my visit with Lance Porter at Russell Tolliver's house, my conversation with Sergeant Mikanopy of the Capitol Police in Tallahassee, and my trip to Palm Beach to meet with Arthur Wainwright. I describe Wainwright's bodyguard. I don't mention Wainwright's wife, Jennifer, because she doesn't seem connected to the investigation. She is a person of interest only to me.

"You've been a busy boy," Cubby says as he has a bite of waffle. Syrup drips down his chin and onto his uniform shirt. He doesn't seem to notice as he continues: "From what you've said, it looks like the drilling bill is the precipitating factor in the murders."

"It's what I've got at this point. I need to look into the American Energy Independence Coalition. They're head-quartered in DC."

"That's fine, as long as you fly coach and pay to check your suitcase," Cubby tells me.

Two days later, I'm on American flight 400 from Fort Myers to Dulles International. I paid for an upgrade to a wider coach seat. Either regular airplane seats have gotten smaller or I've gotten larger. I prefer to think it's the seats. In fact I read a story reporting that the airlines, to increase revenues, are jamming more seats into the cabins. So what the hell, pass the doughnuts.

I've never bothered to get a TSA Known Traveler Number (KTN), which allows faster passage through security sans a body cavity search, but I identified myself to the airline as a detective, putting me in the prescreened line anyway and allowing me to pack my Colt and ammo in my suitcase. If I'd taken a federal training program called Law Enforcement Officers Flying Armed I could have carried my weapon in the cabin. But I hadn't, so if trouble occurs during the flight, I'll have to rely on the plastic utensils that come with the meal, if there is a meal, which there probably isn't. Maybe I can turn a bag of peanuts into a lethal weapon.

I have a window seat in the first row of the main cabin. An elderly woman, who boarded using a walker, is on the aisle of my row. In a crisis, she'll be no help at all, unless she's taken a course called Using a Walker as a Bludgeon. Or maybe she's an armed air marshal in deep cover.

The mind wanders when bored.

I'd called the American Energy Independence Coalition and made an appointment with Theodore Tomlinson, the executive director. Lance Porter told me that Tomlinson has headed the group for eight years. Before that, he was executive vice president of global communications for International Oil Patch Partners. Maybe that's significant, maybe it isn't.

We land at Dulles without incident. I'm staying overnight because the only return flight to Fort Myers is at 11 P.M., not very convenient. I have two hours before my meeting. I cab it to my hotel, the Hay-Adams, a DC institution. I'll pay the difference between that and the airport Hilton, which is more compatible with my police expense account.

I haven't been to DC since my Marine Corps days when I was stationed for six months at the marine barracks at Eighth and I Streets. The marines there perform ceremonial and presidential support duties and don't have to sleep in tents, take long hikes carrying fifty-pound packs, eat canned meals, or get shot at. If I could have been stationed there permanently, I might still be in the Green and Grueling. I thought I looked pretty spiffy in my dress blues, and some of the young ladies I met in the after-work bars did too. I'd have worn my sword, but it would have gotten in the way while dancing.

It's a nice cab ride into the city from the airport, passing the historic, impressive government buildings and monuments in the bustling capital. If you didn't know better, you might believe that the federal government is working hard on behalf of the taxpayers. But, given the opinion polls, hardly anyone believes that anymore. Surely there are a great many career government workers diligently performing their duties, as well as honest politicians in the mold of *Mr. Smith Goes to Washington*, the 1939 movie starring James Stewart about an appointed senator who fought the corrupt system.

But the citizenry clearly believes that those good people are in the minority.

The taxi deposits me under the front portico of the Hay-Adams on Sixteenth Street Northwest. A uniformed bellman lifts my suitcase from the cab's trunk and assures me it will be waiting in my room.

I enter a lobby of dark woods and marble floors with oriental rugs, not unlike the interior of Arthur Wainwright's house, but on a larger scale. There is a cross section of people of various ethnicities and regional garbs, presumably there to do business with the federal government. According to Sam Long Tree, Native Americans long ago gave up on the federal government. Tribes are nations unto themselves and, at least in some ways, including the ability to own casinos, better off for it.

I check into my room, accessorize my black polo shirt and khaki slacks with a navy blazer. I leave the hotel and find a deli a block away, right where the concierge said it would be, have a passable corned beef sandwich, and take a cab to the offices of the American Energy Independence Coalition on K Street, a thoroughfare that is the headquarters of lobbyists, think tanks, and advocacy groups. In other words, the seat of the real government of the United States.

The cab parks in front of an eight-story granite building. The directory in the lobby says that my destination is on the top floor. I ride the elevator up and find double glass doors with the name of the AEIC lettered on them, enter, and tell the female receptionist who I am and why I'm there. She asks me to have a seat, offers the usual beverages, which I decline, and informs me that Mr. Tomlinson will be available momentarily.

I plop myself down onto an upholstered sofa and scan the magazines fanned out on a coffee table: mainly oil industry publications and sports magazines. I choose the current *Sports illustrated* over *The Journal of Deep-Well Drilling* and am just getting into an article about the Major League Baseball season (my Cubbies are predicted to have a good year), when a man comes through the door leading to the inner offices. He offers his hand and says, "Detective Starkey, I'm Ted Tomlinson. I'm afraid, after your long flight, that I can't shed any light on your investigation, but I'm happy to chat with you."

I'm struck by the similarity of that statement with Arthur Wainwright's greeting. I shake his hand and say, "I just have a few questions, if you don't mind."

Tomlinson has greying brown hair, appears to be in his early sixties, and has an American flag pin on the lapel of his suit coat. He could be an FBI agent, except that on his other lapel is a gold pin depicting an oil drilling rig. What's good for Big Oil is good for America is the point, I suppose.

I noted when we shook hands that he is wearing a Patek Philippe watch. I read an article about the current craze for expensive watches in *Men's Journal*. Pateks start at about twenty K and top out at just under a million buckaroos. I'd thought: Jesus, Mary, and Joseph, who'd pay that much for the time of day? Now I have my answer. I'm sure that my Casio runner's watch keeps just as good time, if not better. But you don't wear a Casio if you work on K Street. Calling to mind that Balzac quotation about the origins of great fortunes, I'm tempted to tell Tomlinson that he's under arrest just for being able to afford that watch. But I'm out of my jurisdiction—a fact he reminds me of when we're seated in leather club chairs in his spacious corner office: "You're a bit out of your jurisdiction, aren't you, Detective Starkey?"

"That's true," I admit. "So I appreciate your seeing me. I won't take much of your time."

Hanging on his office walls are photos of Tomlinson with presidents and other recognizable politicians, world leaders, sports stars, and entertainment-industry celebrities. The point being that Ted Tomlinson is a power player.

He shoots his cuff, checks his Patek, and says, "I'm meeting with the Saudi ambassador in fifteen minutes. So what is it you would like to know, Detective?"

Important people are always tightly scheduled. I look at my Casio and say, "I'll get right to the point because I'm due at the White House shortly."

He smiles. "The public tours are on the hour."

Busted.

When making the appointment, I told his assistant what I wanted to discuss, and why. No doubt he'd had a chat with Wainwright about me and my investigation. Moving right along, I tell him, "I understand that your group supports the Florida oil and gas drilling bill."

"Let me make something clear, Detective Starkey. The American Energy Independence Coalition supports the American oil and gas industry in order to help end our nation's dependence on foreign energy sources."

I have to restrain myself from standing up, putting my hand over my heart, and reciting the Pledge of Allegiance.

"I can see how you'd want to move the drilling limit in the gulf in to fifty miles," I say. "In order to keep our enemies at bay."

Ignoring my sarcasm, he says, "I wouldn't put it that way exactly, but you are essentially correct. Deep-water drilling in the gulf is getting played out and is very expensive. We know there are rich oil and gas reserves closer in, so why not tap into them? In an environmentally sound manner, of course."

Sure, just like BP's Deepwater Horizon rig. Immense globs of oil from that disaster still float beneath the surface and rest on the bottom of the gulf. But he already knows that. I ask: "Can I get a list of your member organizations?"

"I'll see that my secretary provides that when you leave."

I have no doubt that Tomlinson has been fully briefed about the murders of Lawrence and Marion Henderson and Russell Tolliver. I know that, if I ask him about any possible tie to those murders and the drilling bill, he'll stonewall me just as Arthur Wainwright had.

In fact I wasn't there to see if he'd blurt out a confession any more than I'd expected Wainwright to fold. What I really wanted was to take the measure of both men: Did they seem capable of being a party to three murders? Things are not always what they seem, but sometimes they are.

After a few more minutes of back-and-forth that produces no valuable information, Tomlinson looks again at his Patek, smiles, and says, "The next White House tour begins in fifteen minutes. You can make it if you hurry."

"I wonder if POTUS is in residence," I say.

"He is," Tomlinson informs me—the ultimate one-upmanship. "I had breakfast with his chief of staff this morning. They leave for South Korea tonight."

Note to self: never try to snow a snowman.

After the meeting, my opinion of Arthur Wainwright and of Ted Tomlinson is that they are either complicit in the murders I'm investigating, or they are not.

Good thing I don't do this for a living anymore.

18.

The Oligarch

I depart our nation's capital with two valuable pieces of information: the membership list of the American Energy Independence Coalition constitutes a Who's Who of the global oil and gas industry, and the Old Ebbitt Grill, the famous DC restaurant where I had dinner before watching the movie *High Noon* for the umpteenth time, in my room, will prepare an off-menu double bacon cheeseburger as good as I've ever had, even for someone with absolutely no clout in the capital whatsoever.

On the flight home, I decide that a good next step will be to research the AEIC's membership list, looking for a company or companies with some sort of connection to, or interest in, oil and gas drilling in the Gulf of Mexico off the southwestern Florida coast. For that research, I need a more sophisticated partner than Google. So driving home from Southwest Florida International, I call Special Agent Sarah Caldwell in Tampa.

"Sure, Jack, I can help with that," she says after I explain what I'm after. "Just scan the membership list and e-mail it to me."

"What's a scan?"

"Okay. Do you have a fax machine?"

"We're getting warmer. I know what a fax machine is. But I don't have one."

"They must have one at the Fort Myers Beach Police Station."

"I knew that," I say.

I'm sure I would have thought of that sooner or later.

Cubby has a secretary fax the list to Sarah as I brief him about my trip to DC.

"What's the back-up plan if this line of investigation proves to be a dead end?" he asks me.

"What's a back-up plan?" I answer.

Three days go by before Sarah phones to say the researchers at Quantico have uncovered some interesting information about one particular company on the AEIC's membership list.

"That company is International Oil Patch Partners," she tells me.

The former employer of Tom Tomlinson, the AEIC executive director.

"It took some digging through federal filings, tax records, shell corporations, and info gathered by our covert surveillance program—don't ask about that," she says. "Turns out that the majority owner of Oil Patch is a Russian oligarch named Sergey Pavlov. He's a guy we keep track of. He also owns Russian oil and gas companies, as well as public utilities, a piece of the Trans-Siberian Railroad and of Aeroflot. Pavlov has an interesting background. He served with Vladimir Putin in the KGB."

"Nice to have pals in high places."

I wonder if Sergey Pavlov is related to the research scientist who did that study about dogs salivating at the sound of a metronome which they related to being fed. Say "doughnut" and I salivate too.

"Is that legal, for a Russian to control a US company?" I ask her.

"Completely legal. Foreign individuals and corporations have been buying up US companies for decades and hiring American lobbying, law, and public relations firms to represent their interests in the US."

A Belgian-Brazilian beer company called InBev bought a majority interest in Anheuser-Busch some years ago. There was grieving at The Baby Doll when that happened. The bartender tied black ribbons around the Budweiser, Bud Lite, and Busch tap handles. However, sales of those brews did not decline one iota. Patriotism has its limits.

Sarah continues: "We also found out that Oil Patch pays $2.2 million dollars annually in dues to the American Energy Independence Coalition, more than triple that of any other member."

"Any evidence that Oil Patch wants to drill in the gulf?"

"They already are. They've got deep-water rigs off the Texas, Louisiana, and Mississippi coasts. A year ago, they got permission from the Florida state government to do some exploratory drilling inside the current coastal limits. They paid the state a four-million-dollar fee for the rights for that. All completely legal."

"Let me guess. The main proponent for granting that permission from the state was Rep. Arthur Wainwright."

"We don't keep track of state politics. That's your deal."

I'll look into that, but I have no doubt that Wainwright was behind the approval process and that Russell Tolliver and Marion Henderson's environmental group were opponents.

"I owe you lunch," I tell Sarah.

"I'd say my info is worth a dinner," she says, and I don't disagree.

That same day, while at my bar, I call Lance Porter in Tallahassee to ask about that Oil Patch oil exploration application. A woman answers his office number by saying, "This is Representative Porter's office. How may we help you?"

"You've gotten a promotion," I tell Porter when he comes on the line.

"The governor appointed me to serve out Russell's term," he says.

"Congrats. Have you heard of International Oil Patch Partners?"

"Sure. They got a state permit to drill exploratory wells inside the legal limit about a year ago. Paid a nice fee for it."

"I'm guessing that Arthur Wainwright supported their application and that your ex-boss opposed it."

"Right. Russell felt that if oil and gas reserves were found close in, the camel would have its nose under the tent."

"And reserves were found?"

"Yes. Substantial reserves which can't be tapped without changing that state law you know about. And it's been discovered that oil companies have secretly been using fracking to extract oil in the gulf. That's not illegal on land or underwater, but it's highly controversial."

"Because?"

"Because highly pressurized liquid is pumped into rock to extract oil and natural gas that otherwise couldn't be reached. Environmentalists say that the process pollutes ground and surface water and can trigger earthquakes. Oil Patch is one of the companies using fracking in the gulf. If they use that method close to our coastline, as Russell believed they would, environmental damage would be even greater. For all I know, they might be using it now for the exploratory wells."

"Did you know that the majority owner of Oil Patch is a Russian named Sergey Pavlov?"

After a moment of silence, he admits, "That I did not know."

"Do you think Wainwright or anyone else in state government knows?"

"I can't say. But I see where you're going with this. The Russians don't hesitate to eliminate anyone who gets in their way."

"I appreciate your help," I tell him. "Are you going to run for election to your seat?"

"I'm thinking about it."

"If you do, you've got my vote."

I've never thought much about saving the environment, but I do know that the Everglades are becoming polluted with fertilizer runoff from farming and development, killing the mangroves. Not a good thing.

The first time an environmental problem affected me directly was in the early 1990s, when the government issued a warning to not eat fish from the Great Lakes because of mercury pollution from coal-fired power plants. My buddies and I used to catch and eat salmon, trout, and perch in Lake Michigan. We stopped after that warning and began fishing northern Wisconsin lakes. The only hazard in doing that is running into Packers fans in the taverns. How can anyone think that wearing a big yellow rubber cheese slice is acceptable headgear?

Of course the threat of pollution in the Gulf of Mexico from offshore drilling is not my main motivation in this case. It is, as it always has been for me, catching murderers. But

I've been living on the gulf for four years, and I wouldn't like to see globs of oil, dead fish, and oil-smeared seabirds washing up on the beaches. I wouldn't want my grandson, Jack, to live in a dying world. And I wouldn't like it if a Russian company is behind polluting American waters or if a Russian hit man is operating on my turf.

So bring it on. I'm all in.

19.

A Russian of My Own

Marisa and I are driving north on I-75 in my Vette on our way to Sarasota for an overnight stay. She likes to hit the fancy shops at Saint Armand's Circle and I've never been to the Ringling Circus Museum. Sarasota was the winter home of the Ringling Bros. and Barnum & Bailey Circus when it traveled the country. It's the second week in April, a good time for sightseeing because the winter residents are beginning their annual migration north and the ranks of vacationers also are thinning.

During the drive to Sarasota, I tell Marisa about Oil Patch and Sergey Pavlov. I also mention that Arthur Wainwright has a bodyguard who is so big he needs his own zip code. "Hate to admit it, but I just might be in over my head," I tell her. "Big Oil, fracking in the gulf, byzantine state politics, K Street lobbyists, a Russian oligarch, and an assassin . . . I've never handled a case with so many moving parts."

"Fortunately, you have your own Russian," she comments.

She is referring to Count Vasily Petrovich, whom I met during that Naples murder investigation.

We have a great time in Sarasota. Marisa buys so much in the shops that the packages won't begin to fit in the Corvette's trunk, so she has to ship them home. The circus museum is terrific: makes me feel like a kid again, with its amazing forty-four-thousand-piece circus model, the parade wagons, the posters, the Big Top, the cannon that shot daredevils through the air, the high wire, the ferocious (fake) tiger and other animals—and the clown car in which, fortunately, there were no live clowns.

We stayed at the Ritz-Carlton, took a walk on the beach, and had a room-service dinner while watching a movie. I suggested *Top Gun*, which I'd seen maybe fifteen times already, but I acceded to Marisa's request for *When Harry Met Sally*, which she admitted to seeing nearly as often as I'd watched my Tom Cruise jet-jockey flick—one of the classics of modern cinema, right up there with *Road House*, *Bull Durham*, *Full Metal Jacket,* and *Hoosiers*.

No romantic comedies on my list.

When we arrive home, I open a Bergoff, carry it out onto the deck, settle into a lounge chair, and make a call to my very own Russian.

Count Vasily Petrovich is neither a count nor really named Vasily Petrovich. He manages a very successful hedge fund in Naples called The Atocha Fund, named for a Spanish treasure galleon that sank in 1622 in a hurricane off the Florida Keys.

I met Vasily a few years ago when he bought a house—if you can call a residence the size of a hotel a house—that Marisa had listed for sale. He invited her to the first dinner party in his new home, and she brought me along as her significant other. It was an elaborate affair attended by a bevy of VIPs, one of whom asked me to refresh his drink, taking me for one of the catering crew.

Vasily's real name is Boris Ivanovich and he is the son of a Russian Mafia kingpin in Brighton Beach, a heavily Russian neighborhood in Brooklyn. His family in Brighton Beach is now mainly into legit businesses, but maybe he can help me learn more about Sergey Pavlov and Oil Patch.

"Very good to hear from you, Jack," he says when he answers my call. "It's been awhile. I trust you are well."

"I am, Vasily. And I trust you too are well, and prosperous."

He chuckles. "Quite right, on both counts."

I explain where I am with my current murder investigation and why I need his help.

"I know of this Sergey Pavlov," he tells me. "He is a very dangerous man—especially when billions of dollars in oil and gas money are involved."

But Vasily is no shrinking violet and he agrees to help me. We schedule a meeting at his office the following Tuesday. It's Friday, and I'm on a flight to Chicago. I decided to attend Claire's wedding, so I'll have to suck it up and watch my ex exchange vows with an orthopedic surgeon who, I'm certain, doesn't deserve her and is probably committing Medicare fraud. Maybe I'll drop a dime on him.

20.

Little Fish, Big Fish

I have an eleven A.M. appointment with Vasily in his office at Atocha Securities on Fifth Avenue South in downtown Naples (he suggested eight A.M., no way; maybe he's on Moscow time). I drive there, park in an adjacent garage, and ride the elevator to the top floor, and enter the firm's office.

The receptionist, an attractive young woman, leads me to Vasily's large corner office. He stands and comes around his desk to greet me. He looks every inch the member of Russian nobility that he is not: mid-to-later sixties, dark hair flecked with grey, matching Van Dyke beard, wearing a dark blue suit and open-collared light blue shirt.

"So Jack, now you are chasing politicians, oil companies, and a Russian oligarch who's richer than Warren Buffett and Bill Gates combined."

"Nice to see you, too, Vasily," I say, shaking his extended hand.

He gestures toward a sitting area in the corner. His dog, Sasha, is sleeping on one of the two club chairs. I take the other one and Vasily sits on the sofa.

"I see that Lena offered you a beverage (I'm carrying the Evian bottle) so let me tell you what I've learned so far," he begins. "Using family connections, here and in Russia, I've ascertained that Sergey Pavlov does indeed have the background you described. He is a member of Putin's inner circle, which makes him especially dangerous if someone annoys him, much less tries to implicate him in murders. There are stories about men who opposed him on business ventures and who can no longer be found. My contacts believe these stories."

"What surprises me about all this," I say, "is how easy it is to connect the dots from the Hendersons to Russell Tolliver to the state oil drilling bill to Arthur Wainwright to the American Energy Independence Coalition to Oil Patch to Pavlov. It's as if the bad guys—if, in fact, they are the bad guys—just don't seem to care if anyone finds out about them."

"That *is* curious, but it is the mark of the men like Sergey Pavlov who rule Russia today," Vasily informs me. "They do what they want and make no attempt to cover up their harsh tactics because it makes people afraid to oppose them."

"Even so, proving that Pavlov and his co-conspirators are responsible for my three murders won't be easy—even with the trail they've left."

"If I remember what you taught me during the Naples investigation, if you can catch a little fish, sometimes that little fish will lead you to the big fish."

"Just what I'm thinking. If I can find the trigger man, he might be persuaded to identify his employers."

"Especially if one of my family members questions him."

"I'll keep that in mind, Vasily."

You could lose body parts you need when being questioned by Vasily's people.

But I'm a long way from having Sergey Pavlov's assassin in an interrogation room at Fort Myers Beach police headquarters, or in some back room or alley in Brighton Beach. So I decide to ask a certain FBI agent I know for help.

21.

A Hacker of My Own

When Special Agent Sarah Caldwell answers my call the next morning, I say, "I'm going to be in Tampa tomorrow, Sarah. Can I buy you that dinner I owe you?"

"Sure, Jack," she said. "What's up?"

"I need a favor related to my murder investigation."

"The way to a girl's heart is through the fish-and-chips at Captain Jerry's Seafood Shack."

"Done and done."

We are at a table on the deck, overlooking Tampa Bay, seagulls wheeling overhead hoping that diners will drop some food. While we munch on our fish-and-chips, I update Sarah on my investigation.

"Holy Russkies, Batman," she exclaims. "You're up to your ass in global intrigue."

"Way out of my depth, Sarah. What would you do?"

She dips a french fry into ketchup. "No offense, Jack, but the world has changed since you were on the job in Chicago. All the investigative action now happens in cyberspace."

"I've heard of that, but I have no idea how to get there."

"How are your computer skills?"

"After some effort, I've got e-mail down pat."

"Just so happens I know the perfect candidate to be your tour guide."

"What's his name and where can I find him?"

"*Her* name is Lucy Gates. No relation to Bill. You can find her in the Federal Correctional Institution in Tallahassee, serving a three-year bid for transferring funds from a bank into her own account in order to pay off her college loans. I know because I'm the one who arrested her."

"Do you think she'd help me?"

"Lucy's a good kid. If I remember correctly, she's got maybe two months left on her sentence. There's no parole for federal prisoners, so we can't offer that, but maybe she'll help just to do a good deed, or to get extra chocolate pudding at dinner. Or, more likely, because she's bored."

"How are her skills?"

"She's world-class. We only caught her because she was overcome with guilt and turned herself in."

So that really does happen. Wouldn't it be nice if Sergey Pavlov did the same? That's not likely, so I ask Sarah to arrange a visit for me at FCI Tallahassee.

～

AFTER SPEAKING with the warden, Sarah calls to tell me I can see Lucy Gates the following Wednesday morning. Sarah also made a call to Lucy's lawyer, Janet Spelling, who thinks my plan is a good idea, providing that we can get a judge's permission for Lucy to touch a computer keyboard, something her sentence has prohibited her from doing for life, and also providing that no one will know that she will do more for me than researching public documents. Sarah assured her that I will agree to those terms.

Google informs me that FCI Tallahassee currently houses 1,104 female inmates in a minimum-security setting. That isn't hard time, but a prison is a prison, and the loss of liberty weighs heavily on a person, even if you're not in a max security lockup with small cells stacked in tiers and some old con singing, "Nobody Knows the Trouble I've Seen" into the night.

Sarah found a federal judge she knows in Tampa who approved my project, or at least the project he was led to believe I was undertaking. Sarah didn't lie, she just didn't volunteer more information than the judge requested. He issued an order, sent to the warden, authorizing Lucy to use one of the prison's computers for the project. That computer's Internet connection is closely monitored, Sarah said, but Lucy is good enough to defeat that surveillance and make it appear she is searching public records to aid in a police investigation.

The next morning, I collect my mail from a box at the end of the dock. I flip through the envelopes and junk-mail flyers on the way back to the boat and notice that the return address on one envelope says it's from the Boyd & Boyd Insurance Agency in Jacksonville.

I toss the mail onto the galley table and open that envelope to find a handwritten note on agency letterhead, and a business card saying that Harlan Boyd is a partner in the agency. The note reads: "Jack, thanks for taking over the case and keep me in mind for all of your insurance needs. Harlan."

Boxers, pro football players, and cops tend to stay in the game too long, and some get irreparably damaged. Harlan Boyd got out in time. Good for him. No more dead bodies to haunt his waking hours and his dreams. I envy him for that.

I head north on I-75 and then merge west onto I-10, heading from Fort Myers Beach to Tallahassee, a six-and-a-half-hour drive.

I turn into the prison's visitors' lot and park. From the outside, the redbrick main building with a gold-domed cupola could be a college, but the "students" are there to learn the error of their ways, and not academic subjects. Graduation earns sweet freedom, not a diploma.

I walk up a flight of steps, enter the building through a glass door, pass through a security portal, having left my pistol in the trunk of my car, show my badge to a female guard seated at a desk, and tell her who I am there to see.

She checks a visitors' list and buzzes me through a metal door leading to another female guard seated at a table who checks my name against a list on a clipboard and explains the rules for visitors: no exchange of goods not approved by her, physical contact limited to a hug and a kiss upon arrival and departure, and visits limited to one hour.

"Is that clear?" she asks.

"Crystal," I answer, a reference to another favorite Tom Cruise flick, *A Few Good Men*, which, apparently, she hasn't seen, or maybe saw only once and so hasn't memorized the dialogue like I have.

The guard buzzes me through another metal door that leads into a visitors' lounge. It is a large room with white walls, windows covered with wire mesh, and groupings of tables and chairs and sofas. There is a table containing a coffee urn, cups and saucers, bottled water, doughnuts (!), and cookies.

Around the room are groups of women of all ages, wearing orange coveralls with the word "Inmate" stenciled in black on the back, and white sneakers without laces (would someone in minimum security hang herself? Never know.). The inmates are sitting and standing with people in civilian clothing. There are a number of small children, including an infant, in the arms of one of the inmates, drinking from a bottle.

I've been in prison visitors' lounges before. They are pleasant enough places, compared to the rest of the institutions, where an inmate can feel almost normal until visiting hours end and their friends and loved ones depart.

I scan the room, looking for a young woman in orange, by herself, when a door at the other end of the room buzzes open and a woman in an orange jumpsuit, appearing to be in her midtwenties, with short dark hair and wire-rimmed glasses, walks in.

I approach her and ask if she is Lucy Gates.

"That's me."

"I'm Detective Jack Starkey."

She looks me over and says, "I knew you weren't Brad Pitt." She gestures toward two upholstered chairs near one of the windows: "Let's sit over there and talk about exactly what you want from me."

When we're seated, I tell her.

"I'll do it just to get back online, if only for a short time," she responds. "I miss it."

"I can't promise you anything in return for your help," I tell her. "Except maybe a CARE package containing a file in a cake."

She smiles, pushes a strand of hair behind her left ear, and says, "Not necessary. In minimum security, we can pretty much walk away whenever we want. Nobody does, or at least not since I've been here, because this is easy time and it's better to serve out your sentence than to become a fugitive."

"If you get caught doing what I've described, you'll be in here longer," I warn her. "Or maybe transferred to a place without tennis courts."

I'd noticed two tennis courts near the parking lot as part of an exercise area behind a high chain-link fence with coils of barbed wire on top. The gate in the fence I drove through was open.

"I don't play tennis," she says. "And I won't get caught."

We chat for a while and have coffee and doughnuts. There is still fifteen minutes left before visitors have to leave. I sense that Lucy Gates doesn't get many visitors, so I tell her something about myself and give her more details about the crimes I'm investigating, even though she doesn't need to know about that. I trust her to keep that confidential. After all, she had the moral character to turn herself in.

She tells me she is from Jacksonville and graduated from Rollins College in Winter Park with a degree in history.

"I wanted to go to law school but couldn't afford it," she says. "I was a self-taught computer nerd. I planned to just 'borrow' (making air quotes) enough money to pay back my student loans from the Jacksonville National Bank and Trust Company. It was easy to hack into the bank's computer system, but, after pulling off the cyber heist, my goddamned conscience got the better of me and I turned myself in."

So Lucy has a good angel on her shoulder too.

"Before the bank job, the worst thing I'd ever done was to change the organic chemistry grade of a friend who wanted to go to medical school from a C to an A," she continues. "The rest was just breaking into secure servers for the sport of it. Well, except for the time I changed the orders of a friend's brother who was in the Marine Corps from Afghanistan to embassy duty in Paris."

There is a loud buzzing from speakers mounted on the walls.

"Time to go," Lucy says.

"The deal with the warden is that you can use the library computer for an hour a day for a week," I tell her, standing to leave. "And then I'll come back and you can tell me what you've found."

She stands up, winks, and says, "I won't need nearly that long, Detective."

So I thought I'd take advantage of what time I had to work on Bill's manuscript. I didn't get very far. When Lucy said she wouldn't need a week, she knew what she was talking about. I'm back in the visitors' lounge two days later.

"He's good, but I'm better," Lucy tells me as we sit with our coffee and doughnuts.

"Who's good?"

"A dude called Peter the Great in the cyber community. A living legend. He covers his tracks, but he has certain signatures that ID him as a Russian hacker who does jobs for the government and for private clients. Clients like Sergey Pavlov, for example."

"How do you know he's a he?" I asked.

"Because sometimes he taunts his targets by signing himself as Peter Alexeyevich, the full name of the czar Peter the Great. He's saying that he rules the Internet."

"So you were able to hack into the Oil Patch server?"

"I was. At first glance, there was no evidence that Pavlov or Oil Patch are doing anything illegal. According to the info that's on the surface, the company's various businesses pay their taxes and follow all the rules. Oil Patch is a member in good standing of the American Energy Independence Coalition. It does pay annual dues much greater than any other member, but that's not illegal. Sergey and his company also make legal contributions to political action committees around the US, including in Florida, in support of election campaigns and ballot initiatives. They contributed the maximum allowable amount to Arthur Wainwright's last reelection campaign, which is ten thousand dollars from Petrov, and another ten from Oil Patch. Petey Boy leaves that kind of info out there as a red herring, to make anyone good enough to hack into their servers think they've gotten everything there is. But I found a path into a secret cyber cavern, so to speak, where the real story lies."

"Which is?"

"Which is evidence of secret payments to certain people of influence in all the states bordering the Gulf of Mexico—people connected to permits and other approvals for Oil Patch projects. And all that is definitely *not* legal."

"Including payments to Arthur Wainwright?"

"Yes. Big money into his offshore banking and investment accounts."

Perhaps big enough to motivate him to protect his cash cow by any means necessary, including murder.

I thank her again for her good work and ask if she wants me to write a letter to the warden, or to anyone else who might make her life in prison, or after she is released, easier.

"Nope," she tells me. "Getting the best of Peter the Great is reward enough."

"What will you do after you've served your time?"

"I don't know. I'd like to set myself up somewhere with a laptop and do legitimate consulting work. But that's not allowed, and I *never* want to be in a place like this again. Maybe I'll be a bicycle mechanic or operate a food truck. I'll find something."

I decide I will try to help her by writing a letter on Fort Myers Beach Police stationery and ask Sarah to do the same on FBI letterhead, expressing our gratitude to Lucy Gates for helping us with an important investigation. We'll provide the letters to Lucy's lawyer, to be used however she wants.

As I'm leaving, Lucy says, "By the way, you'll find three million bucks in your bank account at Manatee National."

I stop and look at her.

"Just kidding," she laughs. "But from your back account, it's obvious you could use the dough."

22.

The Bodyguard

"**D**on't do what you did during that Naples case," Marisa tells me as we stroll along the beach on Sanibel Island, watching the tourists collect seashells. I'd gone undercover as a wealthy member of Naples high society in an attempt to draw the fire of whoever was murdering people with that profile. It worked, but I'd almost gotten killed myself.

When I don't respond, she says, "Jack, you weren't thinking about that until I mentioned it, were you? Going undercover, I mean."

I wasn't, but it's a good idea, and I don't have another, so I want to believe that I would have thought of it, eventually.

She punches me on the arm. "You're going to do it, aren't you? *Aren't you?*" She stops walking and her face clouds over. "If something happens to you, big guy, I'll have to go through the hassle of finding a new boyfriend, just as I'm beginning to have you properly broken in."

"I'd hate to inconvenience you by dying, but I'm sure you'd have no shortage of suitors. Like that boy-toy who takes care of your pool, for one. I've seen how he looks at you. And that lawyer who handles your real estate closings. And the guy who delivers your spring water . . ."

She puts her arm through mine, begins walking again, and says, "Yeah, I guess you're right. But keep your head down anyway. Funerals are such downers."

I decide that another visit with Lance Porter, the newly minted state representative, will be a good start on Marisa's undercover idea. I'll get his thoughts on how best to pull it off. After all, I'm one of his constituents. Maybe he'll throw in an American flag lapel pin and a tour of the state capitol building.

When I call his office in Tallahassee, the woman who answers assures me she'll relay my request for a meeting to Representative Porter's administrative assistant and someone will get back to me. So now that Porter is a VIP, I have to go through at least two gatekeepers to get to him.

I'd appoint my cat, Joe, as my admin assistant, but he already thinks I'm his.

A woman named Lori phones me the next morning to say that Porter's schedule is very tight—"He has a lot on his plate," is how she puts it—but that I can meet him the following day at one o'clock at the Capital City Country Club following his round of golf. I always have a lot on my plate too—but that's at meal times and doesn't interfere with my schedule.

I tell Lori that's fine, I'll cancel my colonoscopy and be there, just to demonstrate how eager I am for the meeting to happen.

"I'll inform Representative Porter," she says.

About the meeting, not the canceled colonoscopy, I assume.

Capital City CC is located in downtown Tallahassee, amidst the pine and oak trees of Myers Park. Golf courses are all sylvan wonderlands. It's too bad that you have to ruin the experience by playing golf.

The brick clubhouse looks a bit like an Eisenhower-era elementary school, a style, Marisa informed me, called mid-century modern, nothing like the elaborate and ornate country clubs in Naples evoking colonial America or Tuscany villas or stately English manor houses.

I pull up under the front portico and turn over my Vette to a young valet.

"Drive her slowly around the lot until she cools down," I instruct him. "She's been rode hard and shouldn't be put away wet."

He says he will. I'll have to give him a nice tip.

Note to self: wise-guy banter can perhaps be overdone.

I'm sipping an Arnie Palmer at the bar. Arnold Palmer, the legendary golfer who invented the drink, consisting of iced tea and lemonade. You don't have to be a golfer to appreciate Palmer's skill and charisma, or his special drink.

The multiple TVs mounted around the barroom are tuned to The Golf Channel, showing some tournament somewhere, and to cable news. Hard to say which programming is more boring. I read a story in the *Fort Myers News-Press* reporting that golf is losing players by the millions as old codgers die off and succeeding generations are not replacing them because they think that the game is too expensive, time-consuming, and difficult and that the rules are far too fussy. My sentiments precisely. There is a bocce ball court in a public park in Fort Myers Beach. Watching old guys play that game is positively thrilling compared to golf on television. "Oh, oh, Bret," a golf commentator will say. "Terwilliger has hit into a lateral hazard. That'll get him a two-stroke penalty. He'll be lucky to take a bogey here and get out of Dodge. He'll finish his round below the cut line unless he birdies the rest of the way in."

Huh?

I'm considering asking the bartender if he can find a baseball game when I spot Porter entering the barroom. He's wearing a white polo shirt with the club's logo on it, and tan shorts with little green crossed golf clubs embroidered on them. Cute as a button. If someone wore an outfit like that to play softball at Chicago's Humboldt Park, he'd be lucky to *just* get laughed off the field. I once saw a guy kept on the bench because he had one of those little alligator logos on his shirt.

There are perspiration stains on Porter's shirtfront and under his armpits. He sees me, waves, takes a stool, and says, by way of greeting, "I absolutely *hate* that fucking game. But a lot of business is done on the links, and you have to be a player if you want to be a player, if you know what I mean. The only *good* thing about it, other than the networking, is that the waiters don't ask your score and refuse to serve you lunch if you didn't make the cut."

"Among my old crowd in Chicago, bowling and slow pitch softball are the games of choice," I tell him. "Both of which are mainly excuses for drinking large amounts of beer."

He laughs. The bartender appears and asks, "What can I get for you, Representative Porter?"

"I'll have a draft Coors Light, Nathaniel," he answers.

Nathaniel hands us menus and sets us up with green cloth placemats imprinted with the club's logo, matching napkins, and silverware. I open my menu. Porter leaves his on the bar and tells me, "I can recommend the chicken pot pie, the Capital Burger, and the Reuben. I've been on the banquet circuit since getting my new job, so I'll just have a chef's salad."

I scan the menu and order a hot dog. Porter asks Nathaniel for his salad. He is served his beer and my Arnie gets a refill. He looks over at a table where three men are having lunch.

"My golf partners," he says. "The guy in the red shirt is CEO of one of the big car rental companies thinking about relocating their corporate headquarters to Fort Myers from New Jersey. The other two men are the president of the Fort Myers Chamber of Commerce and the state senator from our district. I've kissed the car rental guy's ass enough for one day, so I told them I needed to eat with my lawyer."

"I'm not sure if that's a promotion from detective."

"Toss-up," he says with a smile.

The food arrives. As we eat, I tell Porter about my plan to pose as the head of a newly formed environmental group opposing the offshore oil drilling bill in order to see if I can flush out the killer of the Hendersons and Russell Tolliver. I tell him that I have reason to suspect Pavlov and Wainwright, but lack evidence that can be used in court.

He is silent for a moment and then says, "Logically, it should be me as the decoy. I'm taking up Russell's cause. The drilling bill is coming up for a vote in two weeks. I'll get very vocal about my opposition, see if anyone comes at me, and you can have my back."

"That's a dangerous game, Lance, as your former boss found out."

"Comes with the territory. I'll hold a press conference tomorrow and state my strong opposition to the bill. Then we'll see what happens."

Meaning I'll have to set up shop in Tallahassee for a while.

I get Cubby to OK an open-ended hotel bill in Tallahassee. He suggests a Motel 6. I decide to pay for an upgrade to a Courtyard by Marriott.

I've never been a bodyguard. But the Kevin Costner movie, *The Bodyguard*, is on my best-of list. I hope it's available on Netflix or somewhere so I can take another look.

23.

Press Conference

The next morning, I locate a Courtyard on Raymond Diehl Road near the capitol and check in. I called ahead to ask if they allowed cats so Joe could accompany me. He's been on road trips with me and likes them, especially when I order something for him from room service—who knew a cat would like pepperoni pizza?—and we watch Animal Planet on TV. But the reservation agent said the hotel has a no-pet policy. I asked her if politicians are allowed. Without missing a beat, she said, "Yes, sir, they are, with a five-hundred-dollar, nonrefundable cleaning fee."

Gotta love that.

Marisa is happy to take care of Joe. She says he'll make a fine roommate if I don't return from Tallahassee. That isn't my plan, but, as the Yiddish proverb says, "Man plans and God laughs."

I couldn't find *The Bodyguard* on TV last night, so I'll have to go from memory. I recall that Kevin Costner saved this client, a famous singer, by leaping in front of an assassin's bullet. That seems a bit drastic, given my salary.

Porter's press conference is scheduled for two P.M. in the Capitol Building media room. Not likely anyone will try to shoot him there, given the tight security. But I'll attend and scan the assembled news media, looking for anyone resembling a Russian hit man rather than a reporter.

It's a precept of the protection business that someone willing to trade his life for an assassination can always get the job done. And it's possible, if improbable, that the hit man could be there, unarmed, just to check out his prey. If it's Alexi, Arthur Wainwright's bodyguard, I'll recognize him, take him aside, and chat about the tricks of his trade, one pro to another.

But first I need to fortify myself with lunch. I ask the young woman at the front desk, whose name tag IDs her as Lisa, where a good sandwich can be found.

"Andrew's Capital Grill and Bar on South Adams Street is a favorite of business execs and politicians," she tells me.

"That kind of crowd gives me indigestion," I say.

I get a nice smile: "Then I recommend the Midtown Caboose on North Meridian Road."

"The name itself speaks highly of the place," I tell her, and she gives me directions.

I'm not disappointed. The diner is an actual caboose, repurposed, situated on a stretch of railroad track in an industrial park about five miles from the hotel.

I have the Blue Plate Special, which today is chicken-fried steak with mashed potatoes, gravy, and green beans. It has always been my opinion that you can improve any food item by breading it and dropping it into a deep fryer—except maybe the lemon meringue pie I have for dessert. But I wouldn't be surprised if they do that at the Florida State Fair in Tampa, where they seem to deep fry everything and put it on a stick, including butter and Hostess Twinkies, both of which I've sampled and found quite tasty.

After lunch, I drive to the Capitol Complex on South Monroe Street, which consists of four buildings, and park in a public garage. The Historic Capitol Building, as it's called, is an imposing white masonry structure with a dome, red-and-white striped awnings, and six pillars in front. It is now a museum.

I find the building where the House and Senate chambers are located, pass through the security checkpoint, showing my badge to allow me to carry my S&W in a belt holster at the small of my back. Porter's office has given the guard my name. I'm wearing khaki slacks and a black polo shirt with the shirttail out to conceal the pistol.

One of the uniformed guards provides directions to the news media room. I take the elevator to the second floor, locate the room, and find a gaggle of news people sitting in folding chairs or standing beside TV cameras or along the walls, facing a podium with the Florida State Seal on its front panel.

I approach the podium to take a closer look. The state seal has a lot going on: There is a Seminole woman spreading hibiscus flowers on a shoreline; two sabal palmettos, the state tree; a steamboat sailing in the background with a sun rising on the horizon, its rays reaching to the sky. Around the rim of the circular seal are the words: "Great Seal of the State of Florida" and "In God We Trust."

The Illinois State Seal is a lot less complicated. Inside a gold circle is a large green dollar sign with Latin words which translate as "Pay to Play."

Or maybe I'm misremembering. But if it isn't that, it should be.

The press conference—which, Porter informed me, is known as a "presser"—is scheduled to begin in ten minutes. I scan the room, doing my best Kevin Costner imitation, and see there are no refreshments on offer, an indication of the low regard state government has for the news media.

Some of the male reporters are wearing sport coats, or have their shirttails out, which could conceal a weapon. The assassin in *The Bodyguard* made a ceramic pistol to avoid detection by the security portal. I remind myself that I am not Kevin Costner and will not take a bullet for Rep. Lance Porter. Afterward I'll be relentless in my pursuit of his killer.

A woman wearing a yellow sunflower-print sundress that is almost as busy as the State Seal, enters the room from a side door. She walks to the podium and says, "Representative Porter will make a brief statement and then take your questions."

Porter comes through the same door, looking very statesmanlike in a navy-blue pin-striped suit, white shirt, and red tie. Note to self: if I ever run for political office, or join the FBI for that matter, I'll need to get a navy-blue pin-striped suit, a white shirt, and red tie. If I lose the election, I can save the outfit for weddings and funerals.

As Porter approaches the podium, I notice a young man with a scraggly beard and rimless glasses standing against a side wall. He reaches inside his sport coat. I tense, think about my gun in its holster, but he comes out with a ballpoint pen and notepad, not a ceramic pistol. He is wearing a tan corduroy sport coat over a black tee shirt and faded jeans. I should have guessed from his attire that he is a newspaper reporter. Assassins get paid more and can afford better clothes.

Unless an assassin is undercover, posing as a newspaper reporter . . .

Unless, unless, unless.

You can drive yourself bonkers with that kind of paranoid thinking. Unless paranoia is good for . . .

Oh, never mind.

Porter taps the microphone on the podium, as many speakers do, causing an irritating noise. He waits for the noise to subside, then says, "Thank you all for coming. I'm here to announce my strong opposition to House Resolution 0022, which would allow oil and gas drilling within fifty miles of our gulf coastline. In so doing, I am taking up the mantle of the late Rep. Russell Tolliver, who died before his time."

A bullet to the head will do that to a person.

"The drilling bill is being backed by the oil and gas industry," Porter continues. "Oil reserves have been found within the proposed fifty-mile limit, thanks to an exploratory permit obtained by International Oil Patch Partners, a permit which Representative Tolliver also opposed. There is no reason to doubt that Oil Patch, and any other companies allowed to drill within the new limit, will use a process called fracking, which has been demonstrated to harm the environment. Another bill to prohibit local governments from declaring a moratorium on fracking is waiting in the wings. HR 0022 has been reported favorably out of two committees and is scheduled for a House vote. I call upon my colleagues on both sides of the aisle to vote against that bill and thus ensure clean waters for future generations. I will now take your questions."

The newspaper guy against the wall raises his hand. Porter points a finger at him and says, "Erik."

"I'm Erik Blalock from the *Tampa Tribune*," he begins.

Porter obviously knows that, so Erik is introducing himself to the television news audience.

"The primary sponsor of HR 0022 is Rep. Arthur Wainwright," Erik continues. "Are you accusing him of collusion with Big Oil?"

"I will leave that for his constituents to decide at the next election," Porter answers.

Slick. Porter has a future as a politician. After years walking a step behind the men with the power, he is now a player.

He points to a youngish woman wearing a red dress, a strand of pearls with matching earrings, spike heels, and a layer of TV makeup that looks better on the screen than in person. She is standing near the front of the room holding a microphone with a little sign on it reading "WTLV ACTION NEWS."

"Laura," Porter says.

She doesn't say her last name like the newspaper guy did. Presumably, as a television personality, everyone already knows who she is.

"Let me begin by saying congratulations on your new job, Lance, and condolences from the entire WTLV Action News team over the loss of Representative Tolliver," Laura begins.

Lance. Maybe they hold two-person press conferences sometimes. At least she didn't call him "Lancie-poo."

"Thank you for that, Laura," Porter responds.

"My question is," she continues, "do you think that the murders of Lawrence and Marion Henderson and Russell Tolliver are connected in any way?"

Amazing! A local TV news reporter actually pursuing the news. I wonder how Porter will handle this apparently unexpected question. He thinks for a moment, rubs his chin with his right hand, then says, "That's a very good question, Laura. It's one I will leave to the authorities investigating those murders to answer."

Perfect. He's been in office for only a brief time, but he's been a staff aide long enough to know the territory. He could run for president with moves like that.

He catches my eye. For a moment, I think he might out me as the authority in charge of the case. But instead he looks away and takes a question from a radio news guy, then from another TV reporter, and then a reporter from a Tampa newspaper, expertly handling all of their questions about deep water drilling and the environment.

Then he checks his watch and says, "That's all we have time for today. Thank you again for coming."

The woman in the busy sundress has been standing off to the side of the podium. She follows Porter through the door. As the journalists are leaving the press room, Laura hands her microphone to her cameraman and comes over to me. She extends her hand, which I take, noticing red-lacquered nails long enough to win a fight with a panther, and says, "I'm Laura DeVoe. You're not with the capital press corps."

It is a statement implying the question: "Who the hell are you, then, and what are you doing on my turf?"

How to answer without being the focus of a special report on that evening's WTLV Action News program? What I come up with is: "I'm with the Capitol Police legislative security division. We're being extra vigilant, ever since the murder of Representative Tolliver."

I need a cover story to explain why I'm shadowing Porter and that seems as good as any. Note to self: call Sergeant Mikanopy and clue him in.

I think Laura might ask to see my credentials, but she winks at me, says, "Good luck with that," and leaves the room, her spike heels clicking on the tile floor.

Laura DeVoe of WTLV Action News looks good facing the camera and, I can report, just as good walking away from it. I'm well aware that we live in a new age in which comments that could be taken as sexual by a man to a woman are verboten, and that's a good thing. I'm guessing that news hasn't reached my old Chicago precinct house.

I change into my running clothes, and have a nice jog around the capital district, ending back at the hotel, where I shower and call Sergeant Mikanopy to ask if I can buy him lunch the next day and ask a favor. He says, sure, that is the very best way to ask for one.

Porter rings me up on my cell and asks, "How'd I do, Jack?"

As good as any political hack I've ever seen, I think. "You were just right," I say. "Now we'll see if you've gotten the attention of the bad guys."

"I feel secure in my condo and office, so how about if you just attend public events with me?"

"That's not the best way to protect someone, but if that's how you want to play it, we can try that for a while."

"Done and done," he says.

Porter has no more public appearances for the day. I flop onto the bed, watching cable news for a while before being put to sleep by more blah-blah-blah about presidential politics. I've already decided that my vote will be "None of the above."

When I wake up, it's dinnertime. I go to the lobby and ask Lisa at the front desk where I can find a sports bar, telling her she made an excellent lunch recommendation. I don't say a "good" sports bar, because, in my experience, there is no such thing as a bad one.

She says that the best are to be found near the Florida State University campus, which makes sense, because Florida State is a big-time football school. She names several, all on or near West Tennessee Street.

"Do you have a favorite?" I ask her.

"I'm a Florida State student, so I know them all. Depends on what you're looking for. One has the best burgers, another the best wings, another the best happy hour." She looks at me and smiles. "And one is best for picking up girls. Or, in my case, guys."

"They all sound good, but for tonight I'll go for the burgers."

She gives me directions to The Seminole.

I sit at the bar eating a Tomahawk burger, which is a half-pound patty made of ground short rib and sirloin with cheese, mushrooms, onion rings, and a fried egg on top. A work of art. It has always been my philosophy that, if a meteor landed on my head, would I want my last meal to have been a small kale salad with the dressing on the side? No siree.

I ask the bartender if he can find a baseball game on one of the many TVs over and around the bar. He looks to be of college age.

"Sure," he says. "We've got satellite with the MLB package."

He picks up a remote, scrolls through a menu, and soon I am watching Cubs' pitcher Jake Arrieta have his way with the opposing lineup.

"Thanks," I tell the bartender. "Are you a Florida State student?"

"Yeah. I bartend and drive for Uber. If I played football, I wouldn't have to work for spending money."

I know what he means. He needs a job, just like Lisa at the hotel. Players at Division One schools like Florida State have to work hard on the field, but generally not off it. Around the country, there've been scandals involving alumni boosters giving star players gifts and no-work jobs. Some police forces, it is alleged, give the players preferential treatment when laws are broken. And the old joke is that football and basketball players in the marquee sports can take courses like "Underwater Basket Weaving" that are not, shall we say, especially rigorous. To me, though, weaving a basket underwater doesn't seem very easy, unless scuba gear is involved. Balancing all that is the fact that Division One colleges and universities make millions of dollars each year from their athletic programs. Rock-star football coaches are paid substantially more than college presidents. Some people, including me, think that the athletes should get a cut.

I return to the hotel before the game ends. I'll admit that baseball games do go long, an issue that the league is beginning to address by suggesting that maybe a batter doesn't need to call time out to unstrap and restrap his gloves more than three times between each pitch. Purists say leave our national pastime alone. That isn't as heated a debate as those concerning the Second Amendment or Roe v. Wade but, among a certain segment of the population, it matters.

24.

The Man with Two Badges

The next morning, I'm in the Courtyard lobby enjoying a complimentary breakfast and reading the sports section of the *Tallahassee Democrat,* a name which makes me question the impartiality of the state capital's daily newspaper.

I suggested to Mikanopy that we meet at noon at the Midtown Caboose. "Excellent choice," he said. "I see you're learning the territory."

I get to the restaurant first, find a booth beside the windows, and order a coffee. Mikanopy arrives fifteen minutes later, spots me, and slides into the booth.

"Sorry," he says. "Had a problem this morning that ran long."

The waitress comes over with menus and coffee. We scan the menus and order. When I'd called him, I'd told him about my cover story and asked for his help. "Have you thought about my plan?" I ask him. "To pose as a member of your force?"

He reaches into his jacket pocket and comes out with a badge, which he slides across the table to me, and says, in a mock-serious tone of voice, "Do you solemnly swear to do whatever the fuck it is you have in mind as a member of the Tallahassee Capitol Police force?"

"I do," I answer, and slip the badge into my pants pocket.

He looks at me and scratches his chin. "I hear you're a stand-up guy so don't make me sorry about this."

"You hear from who?"

"From Sam Long Tree, for one. And I met Cubby Cullen at a police chief's conference in Orlando a few years ago. I called him yesterday. He said you're worth every dollar he's paying you."

As we eat, I give him more details about my theory of the case and what I'm doing with Lance Porter.

Mikanopy asks, "How much do you know about Porter?"

"Not all that much. Just his basic résumé. Why do you ask?"

"No reason. Just good to know who the players are in a game where shots are being fired."

I get the idea that Mikanopy has some sort of suspicion about Porter but, for some reason, doesn't want to tell me about it, at least not yet.

25.

Stay Away from Windows

Police work, like combat, is mostly boring. There are long periods of mundane, routine tasks, punctuated with interludes of frantic, adrenaline-pumping action and danger. But mostly boredom. As a cop, stakeouts are the worst. You wait and watch for hours and days at a time, drinking too much coffee, fighting to stay focused as you sit in your car or keep watch out a window. Same deal with body guarding, I find out.

For the next three days Rep. Lance Porter has only two public events. A group of Cub Scouts and their adult leaders from a pack in Fort Myers stops by his office for handshakes and photos as part of a capital tour, and he (and I) attend a fund-raising dinner hosted by the Leon County Democratic Club where the only credible threat is the meal which involves some sort of overcooked brown meat.

I decide to give it three more days before heading back to Fort Myers Beach. I'm in my hotel room at nine P.M. watching *The Bachelor* and trying to figure out why it's one of Marisa's favorite shows when I get a call from Mikanopy.

"There's been a shooting at Lance Porter's house," Mikanopy informs me. "He wasn't hit. I'm on my way to there. Come if you want."

"I will. What's the address?"

He gives it to me. I flip off the TV before the bachelor makes his choice (I favored the brunette with a journalism degree from Columbia, but he went for the blonde aspiring actress) and drive to Porter's house.

I'm there in ten minutes. It's a tidy yellow-stucco bunga-low in a nice residential neighborhood. I park on the street. A Tallahassee PD cruiser and a Capitol Police SUV are in the driveway. I walk to the front porch, try the door, which is unlocked, and go in. Porter, Mikanopy, and a beefy uni-formed policeman are standing in the living room. The cop wears sergeant's stripes; his nameplate says he's named Jacoby.

Sergeant Jacoby reflexively puts his hand on his holstered pistol and asks, "And who the fuck're you?"

"It's okay, Sergeant, he's my bodyguard," Porter tells him.

Jacoby looks me over and says, "It was my impression that bodyguards are supposed to guard the body while it's still alive."

He has a point. The curtains are open on the front plate-glass window. There is a small bullet hole in it. The opposite plaster wall has a chunk out of it.

"His fee *is* higher if his client doesn't get offed," Mikanopy says with a grin.

"So what happened?" I ask the group.

"I was in my office at the back of the house doing some paperwork when I heard a noise," Porter explains. "I came in here and saw the hole in the window and the chip in the wall and called 911. I didn't hear a gunshot."

Jacoby takes a small plastic evidence bag out of his pants pocket. It contains a metal fragment. "Dug this out of the wall," he says. "Small caliber slug, probably a .22."

I wonder why Porter didn't call me. He apparently guesses that and says, "I wasn't hurt so I planned to tell you about this in the morning."

"We always notify the Capitol Police when a state government official is involved in an incident," Jacoby tells me. He looks at Porter: "You need to come to headquarters tomorrow to talk about who might have done this and why you feel it necessary to employ a so-called bodyguard."

Ouch.

When Sergeant Jacoby departs, Porter offers Mikanopy and me a beverage. Mikanopy asks for a beer and I take coffee. Porter pours vodka on ice for himself. We sit in the living room sipping our drinks. I realize that I know nothing about Porter's private life other than that he'd been an Army Ranger and served in government staff jobs. There are no photographs in the living room to indicate if he's married or has children. Maybe there are photos like that in his study.

"Seems odd," Mikanopy comments. "A shot through the window with no target in sight. More like a warning than an assassination attempt."

He's right. That wasn't the MO of the killer I'm chasing.

"Maybe this was just a warning," Porter tells us. "After the bill is passed, which it will be, there'll be no reason for anyone to want me out of the way."

True. And I will be left without a plan to catch the killer of the Hendersons and Russell Tolliver.

"Until the vote," I tell Porter, "stay away from windows."

26.

Oscar's Chicken

Porter scheduled one more public event before the big vote. He agreed to be the keynote speaker at the annual awards dinner of Citizens for a Sane Environment, Marion Henderson's organization, at the Hyatt Place hotel in Fort Myers. Tom Henderson, Larry's brother, would be there with his wife, Lynette, and Larry and Marion's children, Nathan and Elise, to see the group's new president present a special award to Marion, posthumously.

The hotel ballroom is crowded with about one hundred attendees when Marisa and I arrive. She regularly makes donations to the group, so she was invited to attend.

We get stick-on name tags at the check-in desk and find our assigned table, number three, which is near the dais where Porter will be sitting. Marisa is dolled up in a black dress, showing some of her front and a lot of her back, and she looks terrific. I asked her if the shoulder holster holding my S&W under my jacket makes me look fat. She said it's not the gun. Note to self: either lose some weight or don't ask her that.

As the salads are being served a woman seated beside Porter stands, approaches the podium, taps on the microphone, causing a loud squelch (you'd think speakers would learn not to do that), and says, "Good evening. I'm Leticia Baker, president of Citizens for a Sane Environment. I'm filling the unexpired term of Marion Henderson and I want to say to her brother-in-law and sister-in-law, Tom and Lynette, and to Larry and Marion's wonderful children, Nathan and Elise, all of whom are with us tonight, thank you for coming and we are all very, very sorry for your loss. Everyone who knew Larry and Marion liked and respected them and we grieve at their untimely passing. Now please enjoy your meals and then we'll hear from our guest of honor, State Rep. Lance Porter."

We've been offered a choice of chicken Oscar or nothing at all. I go with the chicken.

The dinner is by invitation only, but a shooter could pose as a hotel staff member. As the dinner progresses, I try to keep an eye on the servers. The only lethal weapon they're packing, as far as I can tell, is the chicken. As dessert is being served (a slice of something that resembles cheesecake but tastes like the cardboard box it came in), Leticia Baker rises to introduce Porter. She reads through his résumé and then he comes to the podium, getting hearty applause.

Porter speaks for twenty minutes, talking about the important work of Citizens for a Sane Environment in safeguarding our precious natural resources so that we can pass on a nation that is less toxic than China to future generations. I hope that the Hyatt Place chef's recipe for chicken Oscar will not be passed on to future generations.

Toward the end of his remarks, Porter says, "You all know that House resolution 0022, regarding oil and gas drilling in the gulf, is coming up for a vote. I will be voting a resounding no!"

He pauses for more applause and gets it. "It appears at this point that the bill will pass the House and the Senate and that Governor Anderson will sign it. But do not despair. We will go on fighting the good fight together, now and in the future. Our cause is just, and we will, in the end, prevail!"

As he is getting a standing ovation, Marisa tells me, "Your pal has all the moves. Too bad he can't get honest work."

Leticia calls what is left of the Henderson family to the dais to present Marion's special award to her children, who are crying. If I needed any extra incentive to catch her killer, which I don't, that would have been it.

27.

Laws and Sausages

Otto von Bismarck nailed it when he said, "Laws are like sausages, it is better not to see them being made." Actually I have seen sausages being made, at the Vienna Beef factory in Chicago, and that was a whole lot more palatable than the spectacle unfolding in the chamber of the Florida House of Representatives.

I'm seated in the visitors' gallery watching the drilling bill being debated before the vote. I'm there not so much to bodyguard, security to get into the room is tight, but to bring a measure of closure to that phase of my homicide investigation. Problem is that there is, at this point, no next phase.

Republicans control the House and Senate and the governor's office. Porter, like his former boss, is a Democrat.

Rep. Arthur Wainwright is the standard bearer for the pro-bill forces. He and his Republican colleagues stand to speak about all of the positive things that will accrue to the state by allowing the close-in drilling, mainly revenue and jobs. My man, Rep. Lance Porter, and his fellow Democrats, delineate the negative impact the bill will have, including pollution of the gulf from the inevitable oil spills and potential earthquakes and groundwater contamination resulting from fracking.

None of that blather is necessary because the issue already has been decided. Impassioned legislative speeches persuade no one. That is all for show, especially when a cable channel televises them. Porter told me that morning that the House head count breaks along party lines, eighty-one to thirty-nine in favor of the bill, and twenty-six to fourteen in the Senate. Governor Lucas Anderson has said he'll sign the bill when (not if) it passes.

When all the verbal diarrhea has run its course, that is in fact the result of the House vote. When the session ends I meet Porter for lunch at Sharkey's Capitol Café in the Capitol Building. Porter doesn't seem particularly upset by the defeat. I suppose that is because he's known the outcome ever since the bill was introduced.

"Now that your work here is done, what will you do next?" he asks me.

"I guess I'll see if the Fort Myers Beach Police Department has a cold-case file and add my notes to it."

Fort Myers Beach PD does have a cold-case file. The only cases in it involve graffiti being spray painted on an outer wall of the Fort Myers Beach Elementary School, a series of bicycle thefts, and five home burglaries six years ago, the prime suspects being a band of thieves from Miami who were arrested for similar break-ins in Naples, Orlando, and Jacksonville but who didn't cop to the Fort Myers Beach jobs, saying it must have been copycats.

Now the file contains my three murders.

I sit in a guest chair in Cubby's office and put my detective's badge on his desk, saying, "I'm oh-for-one for your department, Cubby."

"Tell you what, Jack. Keep the badge and I'll give you something easy next," he tells me. "Maybe a convenience-store stickup where we've got the guy on a security camera tape, and a bystander got his car license plate number. Solve that one and you're batting .500. That's better than the top ten hitters in the Hall of Fame, who I bet you can name."

"Ty Cobb hit .366 lifetime," I respond. "Rogers Hornsby was .358; Shoeless Joe Jackson, .356; Lefty O'Doul, .349; and Ed Delahanty, .346. I could go on. My dad could name the top fifty. My brother, Joe, and I were working our way there when Dad died, and then Joe died, and I stopped at twenty."

He slides the badge toward me and says, "This will get you out of speeding tickets. We call the color of your Vette 'arrest-me red.'"

I know that Cubby really wants me to keep the badge so I'll be on call for future investigations—why, I can't say, given my performance. I pick it up and put it back into my pocket. Easier than arguing with him. As I stand to leave he takes his wallet out of a desk drawer, extracts a dollar, and hands it to me.

"We'll mail you a W-2 form. The federal government should leave you with about eighty-nine cents."

Fortunately there is no state income tax in Florida. I decide not to submit an expense report for my meals, mileage, and hotel bills—at least not until the killer is brought to justice. At this point, it looks like I'll have to eat those costs.

28.

Red Cloud Speaks

But my next case is not as easy as Cubby Cullen's hypothetical about a convenience store robbery.

I return to my usual routine: keeping busy at the Parrot, looking over Bill's latest additions to the manuscript, trying to watch my weight decline instead of increase by forgoing sugary snacks and stepping up my workouts, and enjoying Marisa's company, and Joe's.

It's nine o'clock on a Saturday and the regular crowd is shuffling into The Drunken Parrot, just like in one of my favorite Billy Joel songs, "Piano Man."

I'm leaning on one end of the bar, chatting with Ricky Mancuso, a friend who owns a small fleet of stone crab fishing boats. Florida stone crab season runs from October 15 to May 15, so we are in the heart of it. I have the delectable item on my menu, supplied right out of the gulf by Ricky.

The crabs are caught in wire traps. If they are of legal size, one of the claws is removed and the crabs are returned to the water, where the missing appendage regenerates. The claw meat is sweet and tender and is especially good dipped in mustard sauce. I like it better than any other species of crab, and better than lobster.

The story goes that no one ever thought to eat stone crab claws until an ichthyologist brought a bunch to Joe Weiss, a guy who moved to Miami Beach from New York and opened an establishment called Joe's Restaurant on Biscayne Street with his wife, Jennie, in 1918. The fish expert had noticed a large number of the crabs in local waters and wondered if they were edible. Joe boiled them and Jennie whipped up some mustard sauce, and the rest is history. The restaurant was renamed Joe's Stone Crab. It still exists and, according to *Restaurant Business Magazine*, which I sometimes flip through in the public library, is the second-highest grossing restaurant in the nation, behind TAO Asian bistro in Vegas and ahead of my favorite place to eat in DC, the Old Ebbitt Grill.

Sam Long Tree walks over to us, tells Ricky we can use ten more dozen stone crab claws, and says to me: "Got a minute, boss?"

Ricky checks his diver's watch, says he needs to get home for dinner, and departs. Sam says, "You know that I'm on the Seminole Tribal Council. There's an issue developing with the casino that's troubling us."

He means the tribe's Arrowhead Casino in Immokalee. "Tell me," I say.

"Someone's skimming revenues and we can't figure out who. We've got cameras on all the dealers and tellers and the nightly count is supervised by a bonded representative from our accounting firm, which we trust."

"How much cash is missing?"

"It started small about four months ago, the best we can tell. It grew until now it's in the range of three or four thousand every week. It adds up."

"Would you like me to look into it?"

He looks at me as if he hadn't thought of that, grins, and says, "I'd appreciate that, Detective."

First time he ever called me that.

The next morning, I locate my Fort Myers Beach detective's badge in a drawer and drive to Immokalee for a tour of the Arrowhead Casino. As I was leaving my boat I fed Joe and told him where I was going. He meowed, which I took to mean, "Bet the red."

I am ignoring the speed limit, not so much figuring my badge will save me from any speeding tickets as just enjoying the drive on a country road when a Florida Highway Patrol trooper, whose cruiser is hidden on a side road behind a stand of Calusa bushes on Highway 82, comes up behind me and pulls me over with a short blast on the siren.

The trooper gets out of the cruiser and comes up to my window. She is an attractive young woman; her hand is on her pistol. There recently have been more shootings of police officers around the nation, including during routine traffic stops.

"Hands on the steering wheel please, sir," she says.

Good technique. I comply. Now she is beside me. Her nameplate says her name is Cpl. Beinekee. The fit of her uniform says she has a tailor who appreciates natural beauty.

"Do you know what the speed limit is on this road, sir?" she asks.

"Eighty-five?" I answer, which is the speed I was traveling. Worth a shot.

"Try forty," she says, with an almost undetectable smile.

"Sorry," I say. "I wasn't paying attention. And going that slow is bad for the car."

I figure that Cpl. Beinekee won't be impressed by my badge and my story that I'm heading to a robbery at the casino which, technically, isn't occurring at the casino.

She smiles and reaches for her ticket pad. As she is writing the ticket, I ask, "Do you come here often?"

Humor still doesn't work. I put the ticket in the glove compartment and think about seeing if Lance Porter can fix it at the state level.

All casinos look pretty much alike, whether they're in Las Vegas, Atlantic City, Biloxi, or on tribal land from Maine to California. Some are housed in elaborate structures mimicking wonders of ancient, modern, or future worlds, and some from the outside look more like chain motels. But once inside, the effect is the same: huge rooms filled with flashing neon forests of slot machines, semicircular felt card-game tables, spinning roulette wheels, long rectangular craps tables where the bones roll, and poker rooms where men and women play it close to the vest and try to avoid tells.

There are bars and restaurants and raised stages where bands of varying degrees of competence can barely be heard above the frantic din of people being separated from their paychecks, because, in the end, the house always wins. Never any windows—the proprietors don't want their customers (aka suckers) to be distracted by outside influences such as the transition from day to night and back to day again. No clocks on the walls. No matter what time it is, it's always time to play.

The Arrowhead Casino is a large two-story structure with tan stucco walls and a metal roof. When I walk inside, I am immediately hit by a blue-grey cloud of acrid, eye-watering, nasal-passage-constricting tobacco smoke. Native American casinos are not governed by local, state, or federal nonsmoking laws. Tribal land is sovereign. Tribes were granted the right to operate gaming venues by the federal Indian Gaming Regulatory Act of 1988.

I used to call Native Americans "Indians" before I met Sam Long Tree. He informed me, in his casual but direct and dignified way, that Indians are from India. Native Americans are the people who originally owned the land I was standing on. He quoted Red Cloud, a leader of the Oglala Lakota: "The white man made us many promises, but he kept only one. He promised to take our land and he took it."

"Now somebody is taking our casino money," Sam told me. "I'm not saying it's a member of your tribe but, given the history of this continent since warfare between Europeans and indigenous peoples began in the seventeenth century, I wouldn't rule it out."

I have no authority on tribal land. Sam hopes to keep quiet whatever fraud is happening so as not to harm the image of the casino. I told him I'd do my best, working with casino security and, if necessary, the tribal police. He'd explained that the FBI has jurisdiction over crimes committed relating to Indian (which was how the feds still refer to Native Americans) gaming crimes because of that federal law authorizing the casinos.

If it gets to that, I know a friendly FBI agent who can keep a secret.

29.

A Riddle, Wrapped in a Mystery, Inside an Enigma

I make my way through the haze, like a fireman in a burning building, across the casino floor toward an information desk. Easier to breathe if I crawled on the floor, but that would be undignified.

The stereotype of older women incessantly feeding slot machines is correct. Some older men, here and there. Apparently the slots attract a mostly elderly crowd, at least in Florida, aka God's Waiting Room.

I pause behind a woman at one of the slots for whom seventy has been in the rearview mirror for many miles. Her white hair is permed into small curls. She's wearing a print housedress and white sneakers. An unfiltered cigarette burns in an ashtray placed on a narrow ledge in front of the machine. It's clear she likes doughnuts as much as I do, maybe more.

Her slot machine is some elaborate game that has something to do with the "Treasures of Cleopatra." A seductive Cleo, camels, pyramids, a desert oasis are pictured. The woman feeds a five-dollar bill into the machine, which flashes its lights: good to go.

She senses my presence, turns, points at the big white plastic play button, and says, "I'm having no luck. How about you try it, sonny boy."

153

I shrug, push the button, and, one in a million, more lights flash, a siren sounds, Cleopatra starts doing a Nile dance, and a cascade of metal token coins pours out into a basket. A computer voice from the machine loudly announces that she's hit a five-thousand-dollar jackpot.

The woman shrieks with joy, stands, gives me a bear hug, then takes one of the coins and hands it to me. "Way to go, playa," she says. "Can you stay awhile longer?"

"Sorry, ma'am, I've got an appointment, but good luck."

As I walk away, I check the coin. Its face value is fifty dollars—fifty times my detective's salary. Time well spent.

There are mostly men playing the card games. All of the dealers are young women wearing tight Hooters-type tops, hot pants, black fishnet stockings, and high black vinyl boots. None of the players I come across are Native Americans. The idea, I guess, is to separate the white man (and woman) from their bank accounts.

"I'm Jack Starkey," I tell the woman behind the information desk. "I have an appointment with Jonathan Running Bear."

He's the head of casino security.

The woman manning the info desk has copper skin and long, shiny dark hair descending to the middle of her back. She is wearing a buckskin dress with fringe and colorful beading. Maybe I'll see if the gift shop has one I can buy for Marisa.

She points to an elevator on a wall behind the roulette tables. "Second floor. John is expecting you."

The elevator opens into a hallway with numerous doors running its length. The third one down is labeled "Security." I open it and enter a large square room. One wall has a bank of screens showing images of the casino floor. A long console with dials and buttons occupies another wall and one wall has a large window overlooking the casino floor. One-way glass, I assume.

A man is sitting at a desk positioned so he can see the screens. He comes around the desk and offers his hand: "Detective Starkey, I'm John Running Bear. Sam Long Tree said you've offered to help us look into a problem we're having."

He appears to be in his forties or early fifties and has the build of a middle linebacker, which Sam told me he had been for Florida State, graduating with a degree in criminal justice. The pros had their eyes on him until he blew out a knee senior year. He worked for a private security company before taking the casino job, Sam told me.

He gestures toward one of the two guest chairs in front of his desk and returns to his seat.

"Sam Long Tree is a good friend. You come highly recommended."

"I don't know if I can add anything to your investigation, Mr. . . . John."

"That's diplomatic of you, Detective. But you're not stepping on any toes here. I'm glad I can draw upon your experience."

I don't mention that I've blown my last case.

"We'll start with a tour of the floor. Then I'll show you the count room. Our general manager, Larry Tall Chief, is in New Orleans today for a convention of casino executives. He'll be back in three days and I can schedule an appointment for you, as well as with a forensic accountant we've hired to examine our accounting firm's audits of our books."

As we ride the elevator down, John says, "We run an honest operation here. The payouts are fair in terms of casino gambling. If someone is consistently losing more than we think he or she can afford, we cut them off and refer them to Gamblers Anonymous. If someone is intoxicated, we get them a ride home. If someone consistently shows an above-average ability to beat the house, which the vast majority of players cannot do, we watch that person carefully. If the player isn't cheating or counting cards, which is legal, but we don't like it, we let that player run. Most casinos don't do that. You win too much and you're banned. So you understand that we don't like being ripped off."

He explains the various games as we pass their areas. He says that the slots are set to a 2-percent hold percentage, meaning that the house gets two dollars for every hundred dollars that players wager. "That's generous," he says. "Doesn't sound like much but it adds up."

We come to the card games and he says, "The best chance you have is blackjack. The possibility of an overall win is 42.22 percent, a tie is 8.48 percent, and the odds of the house winning are 49.1 percent. And if you know what you're doing, you can get along okay in the poker rooms."

Next come the spinning roulette wheels each with a little white ball whirling around the edges and finally falling into a hole.

"Generally, the easier a game is to understand, the worse the odds for the player," John explains. "Like roulette, where the house has a 37-to-1 edge and only pays out 35-to-1 if you win. That's just the way the complicated mathematical formula for calculating the odds works out."

We continue with his tutorial while strolling around the crowded floor, covering the rest of the games. Mostly the players seem happy to be there, even though the odds are against them. Maybe the casino odds are better than in their real lives.

"Lesson learned," I tell him. "Don't bet against the house. *Be* the house."

"You got it. And in case you're thinking about buying a Powerball ticket for that $1.5 billion drawing tomorrow night, your odds of picking all six numbers are one in 292.2 million."

"But there are winners, and it's fun to watch the drawings on TV because they always have a pretty girl picking the balls out of the drum."

"Good marketing," John says as we complete the circuit of the main floor. "Now let's see the count room."

Back on the second floor we stop before an unlabeled door. John punches numbers into a keypad to unlock it. We enter a large room with white walls and bright fluorescent lights that illuminate tables with maybe twenty men and women using machines to count stacks of paper currency and coins. The machines create an electronic din of whirring and metallic clanking noises.

"We monitor this process closely by those cameras on the ceiling, and by searching the workers when they leave, even though I know all of these people and their families. All Seminoles. So I don't think this is where the problem is, but we'll see."

"What happens to all this money once it's counted?"

"Every night our armored car company picks it up and takes it to our bank for deposit to our account."

"Which bank?"

"Manatee National in Fort Myers."

Interesting. The bank that keeps coming up in my investigations.

"I hope they at least gave you a toaster or a clock radio when you opened your account."

"What they give us is preferred treatment, meaning good interest rates, competitive investment returns, and the services of their correspondent banks around the world."

"That's my bank too," I tell him. "Maybe you could put in a word for me to get free checking."

"I'll see what I can do."

Back in his office, I ask him where he suspects the problem is.

"You'll get a better answer from Larry Tall Chief and the forensic accountant when you meet with them. All I know is that the security tapes show no evidence that the dealers or cashiers are skimming or that money is being lost in the count. But our count number has been ending up higher than our bank balance for the last four months. So you'd think that the armored car guys are the problem. But I don't see how because, once the first discrepancy was noticed, I began to randomly ride to the bank with them, but the balances were still off, whether I rode with them or not."

"As Winston Churchill said, it's a riddle, wrapped in a mystery, inside an enigma."

"That's why you're paid the big bucks to solve it, Jack," he said.

The big *buck*—plus the fifty I just got from the slot machine lady. This job is becoming downright lucrative.

30.

Dead Even

The only thing I know for certain is that Reynold Livingstone III, the bank's former executive veep, isn't taking the casino's money. So that narrows the suspect pool to—everyone employed by the casino and by its accounting firm and the armored car company and the bank.

It would be both unkind and inaccurate to say that I'm not making progress.

I'm at The Drunken Parrot on a Friday afternoon telling Sam about that promising and laudatory progress and waiting for John Running Bear to set up my next round of meetings when Cubby Cullen comes in. Respecting the casino's request for privacy, I haven't told Cubby about the casino case. He wouldn't mind if he knew; a dollar doesn't buy my exclusive services, after all.

"You still got that detective's badge, Jack?" he asks me.

"Nothing good can come of a question like that, Cubby. But have one on the house."

He orders a Blue Moon ale with an orange slice. After he has his first sip, he tells me: "I'm not suggesting that you get involved in a new case. But there's just been a murder that maybe relates to your old one."

"Tell me."

Cubby knows that I hate cold cases as much as every detective does.

"Guy named Turner Hatfield was found dead in his office last night. He was a lawyer in solo practice. Office on Canal Street. Shot once in the head with a small-caliber pistol. Cleaning lady found him on the floor at eleven P.M."

"To state the obvious, there's a pretty big suspect pool for the murder of a lawyer, Cubby."

"True. Thing that made me think of you was that Hatfield was challenging your pal Lance Porter for Porter's House seat. Don't know if that means anything or not."

There is a chapter in the *Detecting for Dummies* handbook titled "Who Benefits?" As in, whoever benefits from a crime should top the list of suspects.

The only person to benefit from all four murders is . . . Lance Porter.

Turner Hatfield was shot with a .22-caliber pistol, same as the Hendersons and Russell Tolliver. My cold case just heated up.

I ask my pal Google for info about the race. The latest opinion polls show that Porter and Hatfield were dead even, within the margin of error. The stories about the race also note that Porter represents a heavily Democratic district. The last time a Republican had won there was more than three decades ago.

Dead even?

Could it be true that the original three murders were not about oil and gas drilling, but about Porter's ambition to become a state representative? Had he killed the Hendersons in order to misdirect investigators about the murder of Tolliver? Had he killed again to eliminate his competition?

Was being a state rep, which was a part-time job paying, I discovered, a meager 29,687 bucks a year, *that* big of a deal?

That certainly seems unlikely, but unlikely is all I've got. Maybe the fact that Obama became a US senator and then president after serving in the Illinois legislature had upped the stakes, at least in Lance Porter's mind.

But was Porter actually capable of committing those murders? I recall that he'd been an Army Ranger, so he had the skills, but that didn't mean he was a psychopath who could kill without remorse. Napoleon said: "Those endowed with it (meaning great ambition) may perform very good or very bad acts. All depends on the principles which direct them."

When Lance Porter was appointed by the governor to fill Russell Tolliver's unexpired term, he lived in Tallahassee because his executive assistant's job was full-time. But to run for Tolliver's seat, he has to be a resident of District 78, which includes Fort Myers.

While having a lunchtime burger at my bar I decide that I need to find out where Porter lives when he isn't in Tallahassee and how he is supporting himself on a state representative's salary. I begin by calling his office in Tallahassee, telling the woman who answers the phone that I'm an old friend and would appreciate getting his home address and phone number.

"I'm sorry, but I'm not allowed to give out that information," she tells me. "But I can give him a message."

"Please tell Representative Porter that Jack Starkey would like to speak with him," I say.

"What is this regarding?"

It would be unwise to say, "You can tell your boss that he is a suspect in four murders." Instead I tell her, "I'm interested in making a contribution to his campaign."

"I'm certain he'll get back to you about that, Mr. Starkey," she assures me.

A campaign contribution is sure-fire bait for a pol, just like a bloody hunk of meat in the water is for a shark.

Porter calls me fifteen minutes later: "It's good to hear from you, Jack, I trust you are well."

"As well as can be expected, given the circumstances."

"Which are?"

"I just had my forty-eighth birthday. I can't run as far or do as many push-ups as I could when I was forty-seven, and sometimes I walk into a room and forget why I'm there. It seemed to happen overnight."

Not really true, but why not let him think that I'm losing it, in case he really is the perp. I'm not yet convinced of that, but it's good to have something to do on the crime-solving front.

He laughs.

"Happens to us all eventually."

"I was thinking we might get together and catch up," I tell him.

"I'd like that. I'm living in Fort Myers now. How about lunch tomorrow at The City Club?"

I know that to be an exclusive private dining club. The perks of power.

"How about one o'clock?" he asks.

I'm glad he didn't suggest an early breakfast meeting. The morning coma thing. I tell him that's fine and we end the call.

I don't intend to ask him over lunch if he's murdered four people. My strategy is to engage in casual chit-chat to see if I can learn anything important, such as where he was when his primary opponent Turner Hatfield was killed, and whether or not he has a full-time job to supplement his state salary. If not, that could indicate he has another source of income. Maybe he's being paid in rubles by Sergey Pavlov.

31.

Online Banking

At the crack of dawn the next morning, by which I mean ten A.M., I go to a Starbucks near a strip mall on Colonial Boulevard, just outside downtown Fort Myers, to meet with a man named Thomas Able, the forensic accountant examining the Arrowhead Casino's books.

Able said he'd be sitting at an outdoor table. There are three unaccompanied men, plus a table of women, seated outside. One of the men is wearing a blue seersucker suit with a white shirt and blue polka-dotted bow tie, and round tortoiseshell glasses. He appears to be in his fifties and has thinning brown hair. An accountant if I ever saw one.

I walk over to his table and introduce myself.

"I'm sorry, but do I know you?" he asks.

Not the accountant. Nor is the second man, who is wearing a pink polo shirt and grey slacks. It seems unlikely that the accountant is a cross-dresser seated with the women. So, using my powers of deduction, I approach the third guy. He looks to be in his thirties, with the tanned face of an outdoorsman; he is wearing a faded blue tee shirt, khaki shorts, and boat shoes and is drinking coffee from a paper cup.

"Tom Able?" I ask.

He half rises, saying, "Good to meet you, Detective Starkey. Forgive how I'm dressed. I was doing some work on my sailboat and didn't have time to go home to change."

"I'll just pop inside to get a coffee," I tell him.

I wait in line as two people ahead of me give the counter girl (who Marisa would call a "barista") complicated Starbuckian drink orders using unrecognizable terms like "vente," "no whip," and "caramel macchiato."

When it's my turn, I tell the girl I'll have a large black coffee. She looks at me with raised eyebrows as if she's never heard an order like that, which she probably hasn't, but she gets my coffee anyway. Maybe she thinks I was raised by wolves, or just woke up from a thirty-year coma.

Back outside, I thank Able for meeting with me and ask what he can tell me about the casino's financial problem.

"I examined the last three years of the casino's financial reports," Able says. "I found nothing unusual. Their accounting firm's work seems to be in order. What I did discover is that, starting four months ago, the casino's bank balance on the afternoon of their daily deposits was correct, but by the next morning, the balances had diminished by growing amounts, leading up to a total forty-thousand-dollar discrepancy."

"So the thief thought he could get away with that?"

"I've seen this before," he says. "It's like a credit card scam. The thief obtains a person's account number and begins making small charges, three dollars, then five, and so on until it grows to several hundred and the thief stops and moves on to someone else."

"How would someone get into the casino's bank account?"

"Nobody robs banks anymore like Willie Sutton walking in with a gun and a paper bag. At least nobody smart. Now it's done by computer hacking. A pro would know that a casino has large cash deposits and withdrawals and so he can operate undetected for a while."

Hacking. Of course.

"Any idea who's responsible?"

"No, but I know someone who can help. A young woman named Lucy Gates. I work with her sometimes in situations like this. Legally of course, backed up with a court order."

Lucy Gates. My hacker too.

"I know her. So she's out of prison?"

I'd forgotten the length of her sentence.

"She's been out a few weeks and set up an Internet consulting firm in Key West. Apparently she helped with a police investigation while incarcerated and got the court's permission to operate her online consulting business."

I'm happy to know that Lucy's assistance with my investigation has allowed her to earn a living.

"How'd you hook up with her?" I ask him.

"She sent out an e-mail blast to companies who she thought could use her services, including mine."

I get Lucy's contact info from him. I'm eager to solve the Arrowhead Casino's problem so I can focus my investigative skills on the murder case.

32.

Personal Affairs

The City Club occupies the entire top floor of a fifteen-story office building in downtown Fort Myers. I ride the elevator up and am greeted by an older man in a suit standing behind a podium which guards the entrance to the club. There is no pass-through security portal; he's less worried about weapons than about exposing the members to the uninitiated lest their lack of couth is infectious.

"Can I help you, sir?" he asks.

I tell him that I'm a guest of Mr. Porter. He says that "Representative Porter" is waiting for me in the barroom. How rude of me to not use my host's highfalutin title.

I pass through the main dining room. A window wall provides an impressive view of the city, including the Caloosahatchee River, Pine Island, and the sparkling blue waters of the Gulf of Mexico. I enter an oak-paneled barroom and see Porter sitting on a stool, chatting up a young female bartender.

He stands, offers a firm handshake, and says, "It's good to see you, Jack. I hope you brought your checkbook."

Just a little joke between us political insiders, wink wink.

"No, but I do have a debit card," I answer.

He smiles.

"That'll work. Let's go to our table and have some lunch."

There seems to be something different about Lance Porter since I last saw him not long ago. I realize that his tailoring, always good, now looks impeccable instead of off-the-rack; his loafers seem made of softer leather, Gucci by the look of the iconic gold horse bits. Maybe he hit the Powerball, but I think the explanation lies elsewhere.

I follow him into the dining room to a table beside one of the windows. A waiter wearing a white shirt, black bow tie, and black tuxedo pants brings a menu to me. He must know that my host doesn't need one, just like at the Capital City Country Club. Menus are for newbies.

True to form, Porter orders a Cobb salad. I find a BLT on the menu and ask for the bacon to be extra crisp, gourmand that I am.

As we wait for our food, I begin by saying, "So I take it you like the job, if you're running for a new term."

"Florida is facing many important and difficult issues. I like to think I can make a difference."

He's giving me his stump speech. Time to change the subject: "How will you spend your time when the legislature isn't in session?"

"I've been assisting Vivian Tolliver, she's Russell's widow, managing her personal affairs, including her ownership of four car dealerships. Unfortunately, Russell's son, Ross, has no head for business. He's living off his trust fund in Los Angeles while trying to become an actor."

Is Porter one of Vivian's "personal affairs"?

"Can you get me a deal on a Chevy Silverado, Lance?"

"Afraid not. Vivian's brands are Lexus, Toyota, Honda, and Acura."

"Thanks, but I'm strictly a made-in-America kind of guy."

"You're out of date, Jack. All of the car brands I mentioned have US factories, while, at this point, thirteen American brands are made almost entirely outside this country."

"My Corvette was made in Bowling Green, Kentucky. I've been to the Corvette museum there. What're you driving these days?"

"I've got a Lexus LS 460. Very nice ride."

I wonder if he got a lover's discount. We are halfway through our lunch when I ask, "What's the maximum amount I can contribute to your campaign?"

"Three K."

I do have my checkbook. I take it out of my inside blazer pocket and write out a check in that amount, made out to Porter for the State House, as he instructed.

With luck, he'll be in prison before my check clears. If he's innocent and gets elected, he'll owe me a favor. Being a judge might be fun.

33.

The Family Jewels

The drive from the Florida mainland to Key West along US 1 is quite spectacular, island hopping on causeways along the Florida Keys, the placid blue waters of the Gulf of Mexico on my right and the frothy white-capped Atlantic Ocean to my left.

I invited Marisa to accompany me, but she has several real estate closings, which means she can take care of Joe. Driving along, I thought about Ernest Hemingway's famous six-toed cats. The writer was given a six-toed cat by a ship captain and that polydactyl feline's descendants still prowl the grounds of the Ernest Hemingway Home and Museum on Whitehead Street in Key West. Joe has the traditional number of five front toes. I counted them this morning.

I'm heading to the southernmost city on the continental US to visit Lucy Gates, computer hacker extraordinaire. I called her to say I need her help and described the Arrowhead Casino situation, telling her that the casino will cover her fee. I explained that Sarah Caldwell had obtained a search warrant from a federal judge so that the work is legal. She readily agreed, asked for details, and said she'd get back to me in a few days.

In addition to the casino investigation, I need to know more about Lance Porter's current activities. I assume that his secrets are floating somewhere out in cyberspace, where Lucy can find them.

"Oh, and there's one other case I'm working on that you could look into," I added. "That one about the Russians and oil drilling in the gulf. It's now four murders and I have a new suspect."

She paused and said, "I take it that you don't have authorization from a judge to go after that suspect."

"That's correct."

"Then you'd better come to Key West. If I agree to help with that case, and I have to think about it, it'll be your fingers on the keyboard, with me as your coach. No way I'm going back to prison."

"No problem. Just use me as your trained monkey."

"A monkey would catch on faster but come on down."

I arrive in Key West five hours after leaving Fort Myers Beach and check in to the Casa Marina Resort on Reynolds Street. The hotel, located on the southern tip of the island, is a three-story yellow-stucco building that looks like a grand old Spanish estate.

My room has a view of the pool. No need to pay for an ocean view because I live on the water. That's for tourists. I stopped for lunch at The Blue Marlin Marina in Islamorada, a world-famous fishing village located at Mile Marker 82, which is how locations are designated along the Overseas Highway. The markers measure the 167-mile distance between Miami and Key West.

The Blue Marlin has excellent fried clam rolls and photos on the walls of celebrities who've come to Islamorada to fish: posed on the docks with their trophies hanging from a hoist; in fighting chairs on the decks of boats, their poles bent under the weight of whatever they'd hooked. Many of the photos are very old, in faded black-and-white, others are in color. There are, among others, Ernest Hemingway, Ted Williams, Joe DiMaggio with Marilyn Monroe, John Wayne, Clint Eastwood, and Bill Clinton with a woman who is not Hillary.

I'm meeting Lucy for dinner at Sloppy Joe's, a historic bar on Duval Street, so I have time for a run along the beach, passing the concrete buoy-shaped marker designating the southernmost point of land in the US, which is located at the corner of South and Whitehead Streets. Then I run along Whitehead, past the Hemingway House, calling out to some of those six-toed cats who are strolling the grounds that Joe says hi. I turn onto Duval, and then back to the hotel.

I shower and, with three hours to kill before dinner, put on my bathing suit and recline in a lounge chair by the pool, reading a book I brought along. I'm not into crime fiction. Been there, lived that. I prefer nonfiction, especially of the historical kind. My book, in hardcover, is called *The Perfect Horse: The Daring U.S. Mission to Rescue the Priceless Stallions Kidnapped by the Nazis* by Elizabeth Letts. It is a compelling read, but even so, I drift off to sleep.

I wake up a half hour later and, for the second time in recent memory, I recall one of my dreams. This one involves me being hired, by whom it isn't clear, to investigate a case involving a connection between alligator poaching and meth cooking in the Everglades. Just before I woke up, I was wading in the Glades in chest-deep water, eyeing a very large Burmese python who was eyeing me, for lunch, apparently. I hope I was getting paid more than a dollar for that case.

I jump into the pool to cool off, then go to my room to continue editing *Stoney's Dilemma*.

Lonnie Williams was now residing in the Graybar Hotel, where he belonged. Any other detective in the department would have received a commendation for that work, but the bosses had long ago stopped giving Stoney such honors because they did not want to hold him up as a good example to rookie cops. He was too much of a maverick—but maybe you had to be a maverick to solve cases no one else could. So instead, they gave him time off for good behavior. In this instance, a week that he spent on a fishing trip to Florida.

Stoney caught a flight from O'Hare to Miami, then rented a car and drove to Key West, where he'd spent many a happy time before. He checked into the Sailfish Inn, a budget motel with a panoramic view of the parking lot, because he couldn't afford one of the high-end places where people stayed who were not on the City of Chicago's payroll—or at least not Chicago employees who weren't on the take. The Sailfish was good enough for him because it provided, as they said in the marines, three hots and a cot.

He put his duffel bag in the room, then went to the poolside tiki bar for a rum drink, telling the lady bartender to hold the fruit and the little umbrella that the tourists liked.

He chatted up the female bartender, whose name was Louise.

Louise made up his drink and said, "I hear the sound of Chicago in your voice, sonny boy."

"And I hear the sound of a lady working for tips in yours," Stoney replied.

She smiled. "I get off at six, in case you were wondering."

"What a coincidence, because I get on at six."

Which made her smile even more and say, "Sounds like a plan, then."

Which it was.

A few days later, Stoney walked down to the Galleon Marina in search of a charter fishing boat with room for another passenger. He walked along the dock until he came upon a boat named E-Z-Livin' with a sign on the dock saying it was available for half-day and day-long charters.

E-Z Livin' was just one of a long line of charter boats, but among the passengers who were already aboard this one were pretty twenty-something girls wearing bikinis that were obviously not sold by the pound.

Stoney spotted a weathered man pouring a bucket of bait into a live well, the captain, obviously, and said to him, "Ahoy there, captain, got room for one more?"

The captain looked at Stoney and said, "Only if you promise to never say 'ahoy' again on my boat."

By now it was time to get ready for my dinner with Lucy. I changed the bartender Louise to Barb in the manuscript because, pre-Marisa, I had spent some time with a bartender in Key West named Louise. Even though the time we spent together was entirely consensual, it was possible that Louise would read the book, conveniently forget the part about her consent, and hire a lawyer to go after a share of Bill's royalty payments.

Sloppy Joe's occupies a two-story white-stucco building with redbrick pillars. The name of the establishment is painted in big lettering on the top story, front and side. Inside, the flags of many countries hang from the ceiling. The walls are covered with memorabilia from the bar's long history, most prominently a display of photos of Sloppy Joe's most famous patron, Ernest Hemingway, whose presence looms large all around Key West. Hanging near the Hemingway gallery is a mounted blue marlin similar to the one suspended from the hoist at the marina where I had lunch.

It's the heart of tourist season, so Sloppy Joe's is crowded when I arrive ten minutes before the appointed time of six thirty. A large group of people is waiting for a table, so I'm glad I made a reservation. I give my name to the hostess, a young lady with blonde hair down to her waist and a mahogany tan. She is wearing a black tank top, Daisy Dukes, and pink rubber flip-flops.

"I'm sorry, sir, but your entire party must be here in order to be seated," she informs me. "But you can wait at the bar."

"I've never understood the reason for that rule," I tell her. "Why can't I wait for my party at my table?"

She gives me a look that seems to say, "Hey, gramps, I don't make the rules, so wait at the bar or go fuck yourself, makes no difference to me."

I locate the one vacant seat at the bar. The bartender asks, "What's your poison, pal?"

He is a heavyset man in his late fifties or early sixties, with a ruddy complexion, full, bushy white beard, and thinning white hair. He's wearing a green, short-sleeved shirt of the kind fishermen wear and tan canvas shorts. He is, in fact, the spitting image of the bar's most famous patron, Papa Hemingway himself.

"I'll have a diet root beer," I tell him.

He has Barq's, not Berghoff's, and serves it to me in a frosted mug. During my drinking days, I had a firm rule: no drinks with more than two ingredients or that came with fruit or paper umbrellas. The coolest drink order ever was spoken by Paul Newman in *The Hustler*. Taking a break from his pool game with Jackie Gleason as Minnesota Fats, Newman's character, Fast Eddie Felson, told the bartender he wanted "J.T.S. Brown (a Kentucky bourbon), no ice, no glass." Now that's a man's drink.

Lucy Gates arrives, dressed almost identically to the hostess, but with a pink tank top. Must be the Key West uniform for young women. I give her a hug and tell the hostess, "This is the rest of my party. *Now* can we get a table?"

"He giving you a hard time, Sherry?" Lucy asks the hostess.

"No more'n any other asshat who comes in." She picks up two menus and says, "Follow me."

Sherry has a brilliant future ahead of her, just not one that involves interacting with the public.

We follow her to a booth near the back corner of the room and slide in.

"You look good, Lucy," I tell her. "Freedom becomes you."

Sherry hands us the menus and a waitress comes over to take our drink orders. Lucy wants a dirty martini and I ask for another diet root beer.

"They don't know how to make a proper martini in federal prison," Lucy says. "They use milk instead of vodka and spit in place of vermouth if someone in the kitchen doesn't like you."

I make a sour face. "Yuck. How's the consulting business?"

"Keeps me busy. And I like Key West better than Tallahassee, if you catch my drift."

I do. Tallahassee is the location of her prison. The waitress returns with our drinks and asks for our dinner order. Lucy wants a taco salad. I get what I always do there, "The Original Sloppy Joe Sandwich," as tasty as a school lunch, and I liked school lunches.

As we wait for our meals, Lucy says, "I've got your answer to the casino scam. Took me less than an hour."

I'm not surprised, given her skills.

"Tell me."

"I was able to track transfers of funds from the casino's bank account into a Schwab account owned by someone named Chester Kravitz. He turns out to be the majority owner of the Top Hat Casino in Atlantic City. The Top Hat is on the verge of bankruptcy. Kravitz has been outspoken about the unfair advantage Indian casinos have. I'm guessing that the theft of Arrowhead funds is his retribution."

"Did you find evidence we can use in court?"

"Whoever Kravitz hired to hack into the Arrowhead account is a real amateur. There's a paper trail, which I've printed out for you, that is easy to follow. I'm thinking that, with what I found, Sarah can get a court order to look into Kravitz's financials, and you've got your man."

I raise my root beer glass in a toast to her: "You're great, Lucy. Send me an invoice for that work and your check will be in the mail."

Our food arrives. Lucy asks, "So where are you with that murder case we worked on—the one you mentioned? Keeping in mind that, if anyone's going to the Graybar Hotel for chasing it, it's going to be you."

Which is why she'd asked me to bring my laptop computer: my fingers on the keys, and my IP address, not hers. As we eat, I detail my suspicions about Lance Porter, who has replaced Sergey Pavlov and Arthur Wainwright as my top murder suspect, and what I need to find out about him.

"We can do that," Lucy says. "How about we meet in your room tomorrow morning, ten-ish?"

A woman with my own biorhythms. We enjoy our meals, then I walk back to the hotel under a starry sky, a warm breeze wafting in off the Atlantic, feeling content and confident that Lucy can help me put Lance Porter's family jewels right into the proverbial wringer.

34.

Background Check

At ten-ish the next morning, I'm waiting in my room for Lucy. There is a knock on the door. When I open it, Lucy is there, along with a room service waiter delivering coffee, OJ, and doughnuts. An investigative team travels on its stomach.

I have the waiter put the food on a table that also holds my laptop and sign the room service check. Lucy pours herself a cup of coffee and says, "Let's get right to it."

I pour coffee for myself, select a powdered sugar doughnut, and sit in front of the laptop as she pulls up a chair beside me.

"You don't need to know the technology behind what I'll tell you to do," she says. "Just hit the keystrokes and scroll on the trackpad as directed."

"I'll try to make you proud, Lucy."

I take a bite of the doughnut; crumbs fall onto the keyboard. When I brush them off, I spill the cup of coffee onto the table, some if it falling onto her lap.

"Not a promising start, Mr. Monkey," she says, using cloth napkins to soak up the coffee. "But let's press ahead."

I follow her instructions for the next four hours, with a break for room service sandwiches, taking a dizzying tour of personal, corporate, and governmental websites, scribbling notes on a hotel pad along the way.

Two hours later, I know a whole lot more about Lance Porter: I have his driver's license, tax returns, credit card and bank statements. He graduated from Lincoln High School in Tallahassee with an A average and was on the cross-country team. He attended the University of South Florida in Tampa on an ROTC scholarship, majoring in psychology, rowing on the crew for four years, and graduating with a B average. After graduation, he was commissioned a second lieutenant in the army, served in a number of postings, and became a Ranger, earning medals, including a Bronze Star with a Combat V and a Purple Heart for service in Afghanistan.

After leaving active duty, he went to work in a Tampa bank's management training program. While there, he volunteered for the campaign of a candidate for mayor of Tampa and joined the mayor's staff when his candidate won. When the mayor, a man named Lester Grimes, was elected to the Florida State Senate, Porter followed him to Tallahassee in a series of staff jobs, ending up as executive assistant.

When Grimes was murdered, the governor appointed Grimes's widow to fill his seat and Porter joined Russell Tolliver's staff. The murder of Lester Grimes was never solved. He was found in his car parked in a capital garage, shot once in the head with a .22-caliber bullet. Was that Porter's first kill? Did he hope that the governor would appoint him to fill the vacancy? Did he try that tactic again with Tolliver, this time successfully?

I ask Lucy to help me examine Porter's financial records for the past five years. They show a person living on a state salary, with the usual living expenses. However, beginning several weeks after Russell Tolliver died, Porter began making deposits of ten thousand a month into his bank account.

I have an idea. I ask Lucy to take me into the records of
Tolliver Motors. Sure enough, that company is paying Porter
ten thousand a month as a "consulting fee." Porter mentioned
that he was helping Vivian Tolliver, who now owns the company, with some "personal matters." But he has no auto dealer
experience, so ten thou a month seems like a lot to pay him.

We surf through other websites, finding nothing note-
worthy, and then Lucy pushes back her chair, sighs, and says,
"Obviously, you can't use any of the stuff we just found in
court."

"That's right, Lucy. But I've got an idea that just might
boat that fish."

I return to Fort Myers Beach, check in with Cubby and
Marisa, telling her what I've learned about the casino caper
and about Lance Porter, and Cubby about the Porter case
only.

My next move on the murder case needs to be one that
has worked for law-enforcement people since the Stone
Age, assuming that there were cops and robbers back then:
surveillance. Follow the suspect until the suspect makes an
incriminating move, which, soon or later, he or she always
seems to do.

I need to be on Lance Porter like holy on the Pope.

35.

The Merry Widow

Compared to a stakeout, watching a turtle race at the state fair seems downright thrilling.

For the next three days, I follow Porter around Fort Myers and on a drive to Tallahassee, using one of Cubby's unmarked cars for the tail. Easier to notice a classic red Corvette convertible is following you than a brown Crown Vic. If I worked for the federal government, I could sit in an air-conditioned room and use a drone or a satellite to do the job. Lucy Gates might actually be able to make that happen. Or I could buy a mini drone, attach a GoPro camera to it, and hire Lucy Gates to operate it. For now, though, it's me in a car, watching and waiting.

While I'm tailing him, Porter never goes to the headquarters of Tolliver Motors, which is located in a Toyota dealership on Lee Boulevard, east of downtown Fort Myers, among a line of other auto dealerships. Where he does go, every night, is to the late Russell Tolliver's house. One of those nights, he takes the Merry Widow, who is maybe twenty years older than he is, to dinner at Veranda, a romantic restaurant located in a two-story cottage-style building on Second Street near the corner of Broadway. Interesting location for a business meeting. Marisa and I have dined there a number of times, always for special occasions: for example, to celebrate the fact that it was a Wednesday.

While the happy couple is enjoying the Veranda's haute cuisine, I'm parked on the street outside, eating a plastic-wrapped tuna sandwich purchased at a 7-Eleven. The label of the sandwich says it was made on the day of the week I bought it, but it doesn't specify which month or year.

After dinner, they drive to the Tolliver homestead in Porter's black Lexus. He leaves at one A.M. The previous two nights, he arrived at the house at dinnertime and left after midnight. Maybe Vivian Tolliver and Lance Porter were really having business meetings, planning tent sales for the dealerships with hot air balloon rides and free hot dogs.

Or maybe they were playing hide the salami.

Vivian Tolliver is an attractive woman, but I don't imagine that Porter is in love with her. More likely, he wants her husband's inventory of Lexuses, Toyota, Hondas, and Acuras.

I recall from Porter's military and medical records that, for the first two years after leaving the army, he was an outpatient at a VA Hospital in Tampa where he was treated for PTSD. That condition is not uncommon. When your body leaves a war zone, your mind can remain there. That happened to some former marines I knew. All but one successfully treated with medication, counseling, and support groups. The other vet killed his girlfriend, a policeman called to the scene, and then himself.

I now believe that Lance Porter, my very own state representative, taught to kill by the army, was driven by political ambition and the desire for financial gain and that his troubled mind made it possible for him to murder five people who stood in his way. If Porter is now in Vivian's will, she's next.

I'm reading the *Fort Myers News-Press* while parked near Porter's house on the fifth morning of my surveillance when I come upon a story on page 3A reporting on a televised debate between Porter and his Republican opponent, Mitchell Gordon.

The story reports that Gordon clearly won the debate by calling Porter unqualified for the position and pointing out that offshore oil and gas drilling, which Porter opposed, was predicted to produce jobs and substantial revenues for the state. Overnight polling had Gordon, the Republican, moving up five points, now trailing Porter by only eight points in the heavily Democratic district. Maybe that is enough for Porter to view him as a threat.

I once used myself as bait to try to draw out the killer. Maybe Mitchell Gordon is about to play that role on this case.

Mitchell Gordon is a heart surgeon in private practice. Maybe he sees himself as another Ben Carson, a successful African American doctor with a desire to give back. I decide that it wouldn't be right to use Gordon as chum for a shark without getting his permission, so I call his office for an appointment.

"Will you be a new patient?" the receptionist wants to know.

I tell her that I'm a detective and I have a private matter to discuss with the doctor.

"His first opening is three weeks from now," she says.

In three weeks, the doc might be a stiff in the morgue. I consider telling her that but settle on something more subtle:

"M'am, I have urgent police business to talk to the doctor about and I'm certain he'll want to meet with me."

She thinks about that and fits me into the schedule.

I arrive at Dr. Gordon's office on time, report to the reception desk, and identify myself by showing my badge. The woman, the same one I spoke with on the phone, I can tell from her voice, shows me to an examining room, where I cool my heels for twenty minutes. Apparently, "urgent" here is defined as a heart attack. "Police business" is somewhere down the list.

Finally there is a knock on the door and a tall man, in his forties, I guess, with the lean physique of a runner, comes in and says, "Detective Starkey, I'm Mitchell Gordon. We're very busy today. How can I help you?"

He sits at a narrow desk against a wall. I take a side chair and I give him the executive summary of the Lance Porter story, asking him to keep everything I'm telling him confidential. He agrees.

When I'm finished, he says, "So you have reason to believe I might be in danger."

"Yes. I'm proposing that we work together to see if Lance Porter makes an attempt on your life."

"Which, ideally, you would prevent."

"I'm good at my job, Doctor, just like you are at yours. But neither of us can guarantee a positive outcome."

He nods.

"Just so, Detective. Just so."

He thinks for a moment, perhaps calculating the odds as he would for a surgery, then says, "I'm in."

36.

The Witching Hour

For the next two weeks, I shadow Gordon during his campaign events, just as I did with Lance Porter for his public appearances after announcing his opposition to the oil and gas drilling bill. The doc does a town hall meeting at a firehouse, a lunch with the Rotary Club, speeches to various civic groups, and a ribbon cutting at a new Chick-fil-A restaurant.

He is a skillful campaigner. I learn that he captained the debate team at Dartmouth before attending medical school at Harvard. I asked how he'd "ended up" in Fort Myers, given those credentials. He said, "Two reasons. My wife is from here, and this town is full of weak hearts."

As the campaigns continued, Gordon had closed the gap to three percentage points. If Porter is going to strike, now is the time. There is a third candidate in the race, a woman representing the Libertarian Party, polling at 4 percent, so no threat.

Three A.M. is known in law enforcement circles as "the witching hour." It is the time of deepest REM (rapid eye movement) sleep, when SWAT teams batter down doors to arrest sleeping perps before they know they've been had. And when burglars like to enter houses they know are occupied. And when assassins strike.

It is three A.M. Dr. Gordon, his wife, Laureen, and their black lab Martin, named for Dr. King, are staying in a Residence Inn near Fort Myers International Airport. I'm positioned in the second-floor bedroom of their two-story yellow Colonial on Belle Meade Drive, located in an upscale neighborhood of Fort Myers, playing blackjack on my iPad.

My Colt is on the table beside my chair.

Waiting for Lance Porter, or perhaps someone he hires for his wet work.

I turned off my iPad. My chair is positioned so that someone coming through the bedroom door won't see me, especially in the dark room. I put pillows under the bed covers to resemble two sleeping bodies.

As a Fort Myers Beach detective, I have no jurisdiction in Fort Myers. But Cubby Cullen knows the Fort Myers police chief and the Lee County sheriff and got them to buy into my plan.

A sheriff's SWAT team is hidden somewhere outside. The team has been instructed to let Porter, or anyone else, enter the house. If they stopped him outside, he couldn't be charged with anything except trespassing, and maybe illegal possession of a firearm if he doesn't have a license for it.

If the SWAT guys hear gunfire, they're instructed to rush inside to see who has survived. If nobody shows up, I'll take the SWAT team to Dunkin' Donuts, on me.

Three twenty A.M.

Three forty.

Four ten.

Maybe Porter doesn't know about REM sleep cycles.

I hear a noise.

Not so much hear it as sense it. That's a skill I learned in the marines while on night patrol. You come to sense a disturbance in the atmosphere around you. An intrusion into your force field. An enemy approaching.

Then I hear the creaking of footsteps on the wooden stairway. Apparently, Porter, or whoever it is, doesn't know how to step on the outside edges of a stairway to avoid the noise.

I stand, pick up the Colt, and press my back against the wall behind where the door will swing open.

The door slowly opens, a moment passes, and then the room is filled with the sound of cracking gunfire as a man dressed in black, wearing a black ski mask, assassinates the pillows.

I noticed that they are the popular My Pillow brand, four of them at $49.99 a pop. I know that because I've seen the infomercial a zillion times. In fact I've come to hate it. I'd rather rest my head on a rock than on a My Pillow. The Gordons are going to need new ones.

The assassin's back is to me. On TV and in the movies, the cop always calls out, "Halt! Police! Drop the gun! Do it now!" Real cops, at least those who survive to fight another day, don't do that. If they want to take the perp alive, they hit him on the head with a heavy object, preferably a piano, if one is handy. If it says "dead or alive" on the wanted poster, they shoot.

I need Porter, or whoever it is, alive. There is no piano in the bedroom, so I whack him on the back of the head with the butt end of my Colt.

He goes down fast and hard. He's holding a semiauto pistol, which he drops as he falls. I kick it away from his reach—although he's down for the count and not about to reach for anything. I take a pair of handcuffs off my belt and cuff his wrists behind his back, then roll him over and pull off his ski mask.

"Hello, Representative Porter," I say. "You just lost my vote."

37.

Cellmates

By now comfortably ahead in the pre-election polls, Dr. Mitchell Gordon held a fund-raising dinner in the ballroom of the Hyatt Place Fort Myers, the same room where Lance Porter addressed the Citizens for a Sane Environment's awards banquet.

Marisa and I are there, seated at a table with Cubby Cullen, Fort Myers Police Chief Carl DeJohn and his wife, Tessa, and Lee County Sheriff Clark David and his wife, Sally.

We are served the same chicken Oscar that we got at the Citizens for a Sane Environment event. I assume it was prepared for us today, and is not left over from the earlier event, but I have no solid evidence of that without an autopsy.

When it's time for Dr. Gordon to speak, he doesn't tap the microphone and cause that awful squelch. He's too experienced for that. When the applause dies down, which takes awhile, he begins: "I have a great many people to thank for my impending victory, and I am going to do that. And I am going to reaffirm the principles I stand for, and restate my campaign promises. But before I do, I want to acknowledge some special guests seated at table two, right over there."

He points to our table. "You all know about the arrest of Lance Porter," he tells the crowd, "and about how he tried to win the election by killing me." He turns toward Laureen, seated near him on the dais. "As you can see, he was unsuccessful."

He looks again at our table. "Those men seated there, backed up by their strong women, are the reason that Laureen and I are here with you tonight. They are the embodiment of the kind of effective law enforcement our society requires during these troubled times."

He moves to his place at the table, picks up his wine glass, returns to the podium, raises the glass in our direction, and says, "Gentlemen, and ladies, I salute you!"

This time we get the standing ovation.

Marisa whispers in my ear: "I like the 'backed up by strong women' part."

Lance Porter is initially charged with the attempted murder of Mitchell and Laureen Gordon, criminal trespass, destruction of property (the pillows), unlawful discharge of a firearm, and resisting arrest, which he hadn't really done because he was unconscious, but it was his word against mine. He did have a permit for the .22-caliber Sig Sauer Mosquito semiauto pistol he was carrying.

But Lee County Attorney Lenore Whiteside wants Porter for the murders. The circumstantial evidence against him is compelling: Porter knew that the Hendersons would be sailing in Pine Island Sound on the day he killed them because his boss, Russell Tolliver, had asked him to schedule a meeting with Marion on the day they'd planned their sail. And, of course, he knew Tolliver's daily schedule, and so he knew when he planned to be out on his boat fishing. Turner Hatfield, like Dr. Gordon, threatened Porter's political career, and was killed in a similar manner as the other victims.

But a jury trial is always a toss-up, especially with only circumstantial evidence. Lenore Whiteside, who is one tough cookie with a batting average rivaling Bryce Harper's, is able to convince Porter and his lawyer that the bullets recovered from the murder victims would demonstrate to a jury that it is highly probable they'd been fired from Porter's gun. The bullet dug out of Porter's living room wall came from that same gun, she tells them, proving that he fired the shot through his own window.

The ballistic tests do not show that conclusively, but a number of Supreme Court rulings, including Frazier v. Cupp in 1969, have held that deceptive interrogation tactics are allowable under certain circumstances.

Porter and his lawyer would find out about that ballistic falsehood during pretrial discovery, but before that can happen, Whiteside puts a plea-bargain offer on the table, with a twenty-four-hour expiration date: in return for confessing to the four murders, Porter will receive a recommendation for consecutive life sentences in a state prison. The alternative is that the prosecution will request the death penalty.

Whiteside did not attempt to connect Porter to the murder of Grimes, which occurred before Porter joined Tolliver's staff. The circumstantial evidence in that case is less compelling, given that Grimes's widow, Samantha, took over his seat in the state senate. But Whiteside does meet with Samantha Grimes to tell her that the man who'd almost certainly killed her husband is in custody.

Porter took the deal, with one exception. A big one. He did not kill the Hendersons. He has a rock-solid alibi for the night of their murders. He was hospitalized for three days at—ironically—the hospital where Dr. Gordon does his surgeries, following complications from an appendectomy. He admits that he killed his boss Russell Tolliver in order to take his job. The Henderson murders gave him the opportunity to do a copycat killing to draw suspicion away from himself by making it appear that all three murders were related to the offshore oil drilling controversy.

Smart man.

Stupid me.

38.

The Murder Book

I was fresh out of suspects for the murders I'd initially been hired to investigate. It was some consolation that Lance Porter had accepted the plea deal and was serving his time in the Union Correctional Institution in Union County.

If I wanted him to, Cubby Cullen could use his law enforcement connections to check up on how Porter is doing, including what job he's been given and who his cellmate is. But it's more fun to imagine that his job involves scut work, such as cleaning the bathrooms. I hope he becomes the prison bitch of a sweaty, inked-up behemoth cellmate with bad teeth and worse breath named Mad Dog. Talk about doing hard time. As long as he doesn't kill his roommate to get the bottom bunk, parole is a possibility, if remote. If granted, he might be young enough when he gets out to run for governor, murder his opponent, win the election, and then pardon himself.

I'm tempted to tell Cubby I've had enough of the investigation, as Marisa urged me to do. So did Joe. When I briefed him on the situation, he meowed, which I took to mean, "Maybe you should get a higher-paying job."

In fact, I do tell Cubby that. Over lunch at Stan's Diner, he says, "You took Lance Porter off the street, and that's not nothing. About 64 percent of murders are unsolved, according to federal crime stats. There's no shame in batting .500 for our local crime wave."

"I know," I agree.

Our food arrives. We eat in silence for a while. Then Cubby looks at me, smiles, and says, "You're not really going to quit, are you?"

"Nope."

"Atta boy."

Samuel Goldwyn, the famous film producer, said, "The harder I work, the luckier I get."

True enough, but work on what? is the question of the moment. I've carefully sifted through the lives of Larry and Marion Henderson, thought I'd solved the case, and was dead wrong.

Had Leticia Baker killed Marion, and also Larry, to get Marion's job as president of Citizens for a Sane Environment? It was, after all, the kind of thing Lance Porter would do.

In the absence of real ideas, those were the kind of loopy thoughts I was having.

Back to square one.

Actually, back to page one—of the Murder Book, which is a file containing everything known about a homicide. My Murder Book is in the evidence room of the Fort Myers Beach police station. Before going to the station the next day, I have lunch with Marisa at Captain Jacks, a clam strip roll for me, Manhattan chowder for her.

"Tell me again the main causes of murder," she says.

"That would be love and money."

"You've tried money, Sherlock. You looked at Larry Henderson's bank. You discovered that Lance Porter killed those people to get his boss's job, which led to money from his car dealerships. Might be time to look at love."

She was right. There had to be something in Larry or Marion's personal life I'd overlooked.

In order to fuel my thinking, I ask the waitress for more tartar sauce.

Cubby finds me in the conference room at the station, starting to review everything we have so far about the Henderson murders: Harlan Boyd's notes, the Coast Guard report, the autopsy report, the FBI audit of the Manatee National Bank, a copy of the Fort Myers police file, and my notes on Reynold Livingstone's suicide, which contain the erroneous conclusion that Lance Porter did the deed.

"Finding anything?" Cubby asks.

"Just that my investigation has led to a dead end concerning the Henderson murders."

After reading the file, I go for a run on the beach, looking for inspiration. All I get is a pulled groin muscle. I limp back to the car, drive to my boat, shower, and head over to The Drunken Parrot.

Spring break has ended, along with the main tourist season, so the bar is populated with local regulars. One of them is Phil Gold, a self-described secular Jew, meaning he likes lox and bagels and tongue sandwiches but feels no particular affinity for the Old Testament. Phil, who owns a hardware store on Estero Boulevard, is bellied up to the bar with a brandy and Mexican Coke, the latter of which we stock just for him. He's explained to me that Coca-Cola USA switched from cane sugar to high fructose corn syrup sometime in the 1980s, but bottlers in Mexico still use the sugar. Coke aficionados can tell the difference, he said. Sugar gives a better taste and is healthier, he claims. I've tried both and can go along with the taste, it's not as sweet, but as to healthier, Phil tips the scale at the weight of a pro football lineman. Enough said. Diet Coke, to him, tastes like kerosene.

"Hey, Phil what's shakin'?" I ask when I join him.

"Lucinda and I just had our fortieth wedding anniversary," he says. "I told her I really appreciate her sticking with me through thick and thin, although I haven't seen thin in a while. There was the time I was deer hunting and one of the guys shot me with a double-0 load. And the time I fell off the ladder while cleaning the gutters and broke my hip. And the time a tornado took off our roof, and the time lightning stuck the store and burned it down . . ."

He takes a sip of his drink and adds, "You know, Jack, I'm beginning to think the woman's bad luck."

I never discuss an ongoing investigation with civilians, except for Marisa and Joe, so I say, "How about them Cubs?"

Phil is from Cleveland originally, but he doesn't take the bait.

39.

The Second-Worst Thing

On Saturday morning, by prearrangement, I visit Tom and Lynette Henderson at their house, a cedar-shingled ranch on Cypress Avenue in a tidy residential neighborhood of Fort Myers. A Ford F-250 truck is parked in the driveway and an aluminum fishing boat on a trailer sits on the lawn beside the garage. Many of the homes I pass in the neighborhood have trucks and boats. These are solid, working-class residents who enjoy the outdoor life Florida offers.

I'm here to deliver the unhappy news that Larry and Marion's killer is still at large. When Porter's arrest was announced, Tom called to thank me for catching his brother and sister-in-law's murderer. He said that brought a measure of peace to him and his wife, and would do the same, eventually, for the children.

The worst thing about a homicide detective's job is delivering the news to next of kin that a loved one is dead. The second worst is telling them that we have not been able to apprehend the killer, at least not yet. If a detective can't do that, then we are just men and women in suits with guns and gold shields who drink coffee, eat doughnuts, and drive around in unmarked sedans talking on the radio.

Tom greets me at the front door, holding a mug of coffee: "When you called you said you have some information about my brother and sister-in-law's murders."

It wasn't the kind of news I wanted to give him on the phone. "Can we talk about it inside?" I ask.

"Sure, sure, sorry," he says, stepping aside and holding the door open.

Lynette comes out of the kitchen. When the three of us are seated in the family room, Lynette says, "The children are at friends' houses. I didn't know what . . ."

I get right to the point: "We've found out that Lance Porter didn't kill Larry and Marion. He was in the hospital when it happened. He did kill two other people, Russell Tolliver and Turner Hatfield."

They exchange glances and wait for me to continue by telling them the real killer has been caught. As I said, this is the second-worst thing about the job.

Next up are some Saturday chores: do the laundry, wash the car, take some shirts and slacks to the cleaners, and pick up a refill of Lipitor at Walgreens (can't imagine why I need it for high cholesterol, must be genetic—couldn't be the double bacon cheeseburgers, nothing that good could be bad for you). None of those tasks requires deep thinking, which, in terms of my investigation, isn't working out very well at the moment. Sometimes you have to take a Zen approach to problem solving: clear the mind and let the answer come to you.

I can report that my mind is, in fact, clear, but the answer is showing no sign of appearing. Maybe I should don a saffron-colored robe and sit cross-legged in a mountain cave, breathing deeply and chanting. But I don't know where to get a robe like that and there are no mountain caves in Florida, so I go back to work on *Stoney's Dilemma*. The world of fiction is often preferable to real life.

Stoney's Key West fishing trip was all catch and release. Now, back on the job in Chicago, that goal had changed. In Stoney's opinion, you only released a perp when the criminal justice system malfunctioned.

"Nice tan, Jack. Now it's time to get your head back in the game."

This said by Lt. Davey Davis, the Homicide Division commander, a tall and lean man in his fifties who always wore impeccably tailored suits, as he found Stoney in the break room, pouring a mug of burned coffee. There was a doughnut box on the counter, inhabited only by crumbs.

Stoney looked at the box.

"Early birds get the pastries," Davis said.

"You being one of them, loot," Stoney replied. "You got powdered sugar on your shirt."

"Why I'm your boss. I start my day before ten."

"So what's new while I was gone?"

"Same old. More shootings on the South Side than during a comparable period in Afghanistan combat."

Davis poured his own mug of coffee. "You talked to your partner yet?"

"I told Bobby I'd get with him right after this."

Davis took a sip of coffee and made a sour face. "Next time, we hire a barista for a secretary instead of a pretty girl. Any who, you and Delahanty are assigned to the murder of a priest."

Stoney left the break room and went to his desk in the squad room. Bobby Delahanty sat at an adjacent desk, feet up, reading the Trib. *Bobby, who was five years older and twenty pounds heavier than Stoney, also had powdered sugar on his shirt front.*

"Anything about the deceased padre in the paper?" Stoney asked his partner.

Bobby put down the paper and sat up. "Page one. It seems that Father Bernard Jacoby of Saint Mary's Parish was found yesterday afternoon in the concession booth . . ."

"That's a confession booth, aka confessional. A concession booth is where they sell beer and hot dogs at Wrigley. When's the last time you were in a church?"

"Not since my mother's funeral service. As I was saying before being so rudely interrupted, the priest was found by a cleaning lady in whatever that box is called, shot three times in the chest. Clearly by someone in the opposite side, given the three bullet holes in the partition."

"Hhmm," Stoney said. "So if the doer had no sins to confess on the way in, he definitely did on the way out. Any leads?"

"The Trib *story notes that the good father had been accused of sexually abusing altar boys in a parish in South Dakota. Never charged, but the church paid the families an undisclosed amount of hush money."*

"How long ago?"

"Eight years. Jacoby did a year in one of those rehab centers the church runs, this one in Arizona, and had been at Saint Mary's ever since."

"I thought the church didn't give pedophiles another shot," Stoney said. "Maybe, due to the shortage of men of the cloth, not to mention nuns, they're changing that."

"Remember the case in Joliet some years ago? An altar boy grew up, did a stint in the Marine Corps, came home and gutted his former parish priest with a combat knife? Claimed the priest had abused him."

"Yeah," Stoney said. "So maybe a trip to South Dakota is in order."

"If nothing else, we could see Mount Rushmore," Delahanty said.

Without having been to Mount Rushmore, my uninformed opinion is, you've been there once, you've been there one too many times. But maybe I'm wrong about that. At any rate, I didn't have to head to the Black Hills of South Dakota to get back to the mystery of the Hendersons' deaths.

What I know so far, or think I know, is that the Henderson murders are apparently not related to Larry's connection to the Manatee National Bank or to Marion's activities as an environmentalist. I realize that I haven't dug very deeply into their personal lives after thinking I'd solved the case.

I decide to start with Larry. During the next week I reinterview the Hendersons' neighbors and an updated list of Larry's friends provided by Tom Henderson, and also the pastor at the church the Hendersons regularly attended. Larry and Marion helped build Habitat for Humanity houses. He did not serve in the military, attended weekly Kiwanis Club meetings, was active in the University of Florida alumni organization, liked to fish, and coached his son Nathan's Little League team.

Well, that was new information. I guess Tom forgot to put that team on the list the first time around.

And, as it turned out, it was while interviewing that team's assistant coach, a man named Hector Diaz, that I learned the father of one of the players had threatened Larry for not playing his son enough.

"We didn't take the threat seriously," Hector tells me when I visit him at the auto body shop he owns in Fort Myers. "When you get involved in youth sports, that kind of thing isn't unusual. Some parents become irate if they think their son or daughter is spending too much time on the bench during baseball or basketball games or soccer matches. The kids don't seem to mind, it's the parents. It makes you sorry you took a coaching job."

"Who's the father?" I ask Hector as we stand beside a Toyota Celica that's been involved in an accident.

"A guy named Alex Kramer. He's a fishing guide."

"What was the threat?"

"After one of our games, Kramer approached Larry in the parking lot. I was just getting into my truck nearby. I couldn't hear what he was saying, but he was shouting and poking his finger into Larry's chest. Later Larry told me that Kramer said Larry was favoring his own son over Kramer's, they both played center field, and that Larry would regret it if he didn't give his kid equal playing time."

"Was that true, about the playing time?"

"I don't really know. I mainly work with the pitchers and catchers and organize the schedule. I don't pay much attention to how often other players are rotated."

"Where can I find Kramer?"

"I don't know where he lives, but he keeps his boat at Turtle Key Marina. It's a Boston Whaler, I think."

40.

Captain Kramer

Turtle Key Marina is located in Cape Coral, a city just west of Fort Myers on the gulf. The marina's main building is a corrugated-metal Quonset-type structure. There is a large shed for inside boat storage and four long docks. There is something familiar about this marina, but I don't know why. I've never been here and I don't know anyone who keeps a boat here.

I enter the building and ask a woman who is stocking shelves with marine motor oil where I can find Alex Kramer.

"Captain Kramer's out on a morning charter," she tells me. "Should be back about one." She looks at the counter and adds, "His card's over there if you want to book a charter."

That's two hours from now. I thank her, take one of the business cards, and drive back to Fort Myers Beach to see Cubby Cullen.

"Sounds promising," Cubby says when I tell him about Kramer and the threat. "I suppose you could take over as coach of that team, bench Kramer's kid, and see what he does."

He's smiling when he says that—not serious.

"What are you really going to do, Jack?"

I take Kramer's card out of my pocket and put it on Cubby's desk. The card has a drawing of a tarpon and Kramer's name and contact info.

"I think I'll do some fishing."

That night Marisa prepares one of her gourmet meals for me and I tell her the latest about the case.

"Wasn't there something like that involving cheerleading?"

I'd read about that case. "A woman in Texas tried to hire a hit man to kill the mother of her daughter's junior high school cheerleading rival. The man she tried to hire turned her in."

"What happened to her?"

"As I recall, she got ten years in prison but only served six months, with the rest on probation. She also had to pay a ton of cash to the family to settle a civil suit."

"I remember that," Marisa says. "There was a movie about the case starring Holly Hunter."

"Yeah, and a TV movie and a novel."

"I saw the movie but didn't read the book."

Note to self: don't go into the book publishing business.

The next morning, I call the number on Kramer's business card. He answers on the fourth ring.

"Captain Kramer," he says. "What can I do for you?"

"I'd like to book a fishing trip," I tell him.

"Sure. I'm fishing the flats with a customer right now. Let me check my book."

He's gone for a minute or two, then says, "I'm pretty busy this time of year, but I had a cancellation for Wednesday morning, if that works."

"Okay. What time?"

"Meet me at the marina at seven."

I was afraid of that.

"Got anything in the afternoon?"

"No, that's it for the next two weeks."

"Okay then, Wednesday morning it is. How're they biting?"

"Getting some good snook, redfish, and snapper," he says.

There's a pause, then he says, "Gotta go, customer just hooked something big."

Just like I hope to do on Wednesday.

I pull into the marina at ten to seven. I witnessed the eastern sunrise on the way over, something I haven't seen since my Marine Corps days. Okay, more recently than that, but I hope to not see it again anytime soon.

I park and enter the marina building. The same woman is standing behind the counter, ringing up a purchase for a male customer. A man is scooping minnows out of a large aeration tank. He is tall and sinewy, built like a rodeo cowboy, and wearing a baseball cap that says "Rapala," a brand of fishing lures, a black tee shirt, jeans, and worn boat shoes. He has sunglasses pushed up on top of the hat and is deeply tanned on his face, neck, and arms.

I walk over and say, "Captain Kramer?"

He nods at me. "The snapper were biting on these yesterday. We'll take some leeches and earthworms along too and go to lures if those don't produce."

I offer my hand and say, "Jack Starkey."

"Figured that," he answers, returning the handshake. He finishes with the minnows, takes two containers out of a cooler on the wall near the counter, and says to the woman, "On my account, Alice."

"Good luck, Alex," she answers as she turns to stack cigarettes in a rack behind the counter.

I follow Kramer outside and down onto one of the docks. He steps aboard a Boston Whaler skiff with a Yamaha outboard, puts the minnow bucket and containers onto the deck, and offers me a hand. Do I look too old to make my own way onto a boat?

Kramer appears to be about my same age, late forties, but I outweigh him by maybe thirty pounds, so I don't take his offer of help as an insult. I step aboard without help as he attends to the mooring lines, sits in the captain's chair, starts the outboard, pulls away from the dock, and says, "We'll try some spots I know in Matlacha Pass that were hitting yesterday, and then maybe go into the river, depending."

I take the chair beside him and say, "You know best, Captain."

He looks at me and says, "I believe that I do—at least out here on the saltwater."

I'd asked Cubby to have someone run a background check on Kramer: married, one son, some arrests over the years for fighting in bars, with fines but no jail time, no felonies. Graduated from Cape Coral High School, did a stint in the Coast Guard, serving in Alaska and Washington State. Active in the American Legion and a dues-paying member of the NRA.

The report didn't say "cold-blooded killer." That was up to me to fill in.

We're drifting in the pass, casting minnows toward mangroves. When Kramer took the poles out of a locker under a seat I saw a shotgun in there. Not unusual to have a weapon on a boat. If it had been a .22-caliber semiauto pistol with a suppressor on the barrel, it might have given me pause. I was wearing my S&W in a belt holster hidden by my untucked tee shirt.

"You live down here, or just visiting?" he asks.

"I was a commodities trader in Chicago," I answer. "Got tired of the stress so I moved to Fort Myers Beach, where I own a bar."

"Which one? Been in most of them, if not all."

He has been in The Drunken Parrot, he says, but isn't a regular or I'd have recognized him.

He hooks a nice redfish, boats it, and asks, "Keep or catch and release?"

"I'll keep that one."

I'm thinking of how Marisa will prepare it for us. He puts it in an ice cooler.

The charter runs from seven to eleven. We fish the pass and then the Caloosahatchee River and together boat four more redfish, a snook, and a sheepshead, switching to leeches in the river. I only need the one snapper for dinner and tell Kramer he can keep any of the rest he wants.

"Thanks, but I don't like fish," he says. "I'm strictly meat and potatoes and fried chicken." So they are all released.

He sees me giving him a look—a fishing guide who doesn't like fish?—and adds, "Don't have to like 'em to know how to catch 'em."

Back at the marina, Kramer cleans my redfish at a metal table on the dock, puts the fillets in a plastic bag with ice, and we go to the marina building, where I pay him his fee of $300 plus a $20 tip because of the good catch.

"Just give me a call if you want to go out again," he says, "and tell your friends."

I assure him I will, but maybe the next time I see him it won't be to fish, it will be to arrest him for the murder of Larry and Marion Henderson. I didn't get a sense of whether he could or could not be the killer during the fishing trip. There is no "look" for someone like that. When interviewed by police, the neighbors of a serial killer with bodies buried in the basement or under the tulips inevitably say, "He seemed like such a nice young man. Always polite and kind to animals and children."

If Kramer doesn't have an alibi for the evening of the Henderson murders, that is only the vaguest of circumstantial evidence. And how did he know that the couple would be out on their boat, and where to find them?

Maybe he'll have a bout of conscience and walk into the police station and confess.

41.

Game Day

It is an unspoken understanding between Hector Diaz and me that I am following up on his comments about Alex Kramer when I call to ask the day and time of the team's next game.

The Fort Myers area Little League teams are named for MLB clubs. Diaz's Marlins were playing the Tampa Bay Rays on Saturday morning at a field near a small airport named Page Field. The Marlins had been given a good spanking by the Cubs during their last game, Diaz told me. Apparently the success of the big club has a trickle-down effect.

I arrive at the ballpark after the game has started, spot Kramer sitting in the bleachers, and take the seat beside him.

"You got a boy on the Tampa Bay Rays?" he asks me. He's drinking a can of Rolling Rock.

I nod toward the Tampa Bay Ray's bench and say, "That's my nephew, Sam. His father couldn't make it today."

"My boy Teddy's in center field."

So Diaz, who just inherited the head coaching job, now is playing the boy. Wise move. Teddy is short and pudgy. When it's time for his team to bat, he takes a very long time to make it to the bench.

We watch the game for a while. I notice that there is a wooden shed behind the bleachers selling food and ask Kramer if I can get him a hot dog. He says sure, and I bring back two dogs and a diet root beer for me. As we're munching, I say, "You know, my brother, Sam's dad, is aggravated about the playing time Sam's getting."

Bait's in the water. Will Kramer bite?

"That's a bitch," he says. "That coach should be horse-whipped."

"Anything like that ever happen on your team?" I ask.

He shakes his head. "Nah, our coach is pretty good about that."

Meaning Hector Diaz—now that Larry Henderson is out of the way? But how to prove that? I'm going to ask Hector to bench Kramer's kid to see if Kramer makes a run at him, in the way that I got Lance Porter to assassinate Mitchell Gordon's My Pillows.

A high fly ball is hit toward center field. Teddy Kramer stares up at it and stands transfixed, as if watching a comet that has nothing to do with him. The left fielder runs hard and catches the ball as it descends about ten feet from Teddy.

"He lost it in the sun," Kramer says.

The sky is overcast with a thick layer of low-hanging grey clouds. By the end of the seventh inning, the Marlins are ahead, twelve runs to none. The umpire invokes a statute-of-limitations rule and ends the game.

∾

THE NEXT morning, while running along the beach, I remember that something had struck me about Turtle Key Marina, but I still don't know why. Kramer works his guide business out of the marina and he is now my main suspect.

After my run, I drive straight to Fort Myers Beach PD headquarters, get the murder book from the property clerk, and head for the conference room.

I encounter Cubby in the hallway. "Are you going undercover as a distance runner?" he asks.

I'm wearing a sweat-drenched tee shirt, shorts, and running shoes. "I didn't know you have a dress code."

"We don't, but we do have a smell code, and you just flunked it."

Ignoring that, I hold up the murder book and say, "There may be something in here I've overlooked."

"Get to it, then, but I'd suggest a shower and change of clothes as next on your to-do list."

I nod and sit in the conference room leafing through the book. Everything is familiar. But then, in one of the Coast Guard reports, I see that the Hendersons kept their sailboat, the *Joie de Vivre*, at Turtle Key Marina. That's why it seemed familiar. I guess Harlan Boyd was already out the door when he said he'd check out where the Hendersons kept the boat, and if anyone had seen anything the night they were killed. That's why we never heard any more about this.

I've already established a connection between Kramer and Larry Henderson from the baseball team. But now I see that there is a way Kramer could have known that the Hendersons were going sailing on the night they were murdered. He might have followed them to Pine Island Sound from the marina, or maybe he was out there with a charter, spotted the boat, told his customer they had to cut the trip short for some invented reason, and gone back to the sound alone.

I call the marina on my cell phone from the conference room. A woman answers who is probably the one I saw manning the counter. I identify myself as a detective, tell her I'm pursuing an unspecified investigation, and ask if the marina keeps a log of the comings and goings of the boats docked there.

"No, we don't do that," she tells me. "If a boat is in dry storage, the owner calls to tell us to put it in the water. If it's kept at the dock, the owners just take it out. Either way, we don't keep a record."

I thank her and end the call.

Sometimes, if you have no solid evidence on a suspect, you can get him to make a mistake by shaking him up. I go back to my boat, find Kramer's business card, and dial his number after entering the code that blocks my number on his caller ID.

"This is Alex Kramer," he says when answering on the first ring. "How can I help you?"

"I know what you did, Alex," I tell him, disguising my voice as best I can.

"Pardon me?"

"I know you killed Lawrence and Marion Henderson."

"Who the hell is this?" Kramer demands.

"Your worst nightmare," I answer. I think a character in a movie I saw said that.

"You know nothing like that. If you did, you'd have gone to the police."

Which isn't a denial. "I didn't because I think we can settle this man-to-man."

"Whataya think you know?"

"I know that you went out on Pine Island Sound, tracked down the Hendersons on their sailboat, went aboard, and shot them each once in the head with a .22-caliber pistol."

He is silent, then says, "I have no reason to kill anybody."

His tone has gone from surprise to anger to subdued. I continue: "How's your son's Little League team doing? The Marlins."

After a moment, he says, "Tell me what you want, asshole."

"I'd really like a nice fishing boat, just like your Whaler. What'd that cost? Twenty, thirty thou, fully rigged?"

"Maybe we can work something out," he says.

Which an innocent man would never say. Kramer is thinking maybe I'm stupid enough to meet him somewhere secluded for a cash handoff so he can kill me.

Which is just what I have in mind, without the killing part.

"Let's do thirty grand," Kramer says. "They'll throw in a trailer for that."

42.

Showdown at the Fruit Stand

Florida is one of eleven states that require two-party consent to record a phone call. Illinois is another. Otherwise I could have pressed Kramer more and maybe have his recorded confession to the Henderson murders. Even without a direct confession, his agreeing to pay me thirty grand in hush money would have been enough to get a search warrant to look for evidence, such as the .22-caliber pistol he used for the killings. And I know where I would have told them to look.

Absent a recording, I instructed him to meet me at eight o'clock at a secluded location off Immokalee Road at a fruit stand in front of an orange grove. Marisa and I have been there a number of times to buy oranges. The stand also sells homemade fruit pies. I haven't had one of those excellent pies in a while, so, if I was meeting anyone but a suspected killer, I would have set the get-together for daytime, when the stand is open.

I'm having lunch with Marisa at Mama Gina's, an Italian restaurant we like on Bonita Beach Road. During the course of the meal, I casually mention that I'm meeting Alex Kramer in a few hours, and why.

She puts her fork down in midbite and gives me a look that could melt the varnish off a century-old church pew.

"So this is maybe a farewell lunch?" she asks.

"No, no, nothing like that. I'm just keeping you up to date on the case. As a courtesy."

"And courteously letting me know that you might be killed so I can take care of Joe, notify your family and business associates, make the final arrangements . . . By the way, do you prefer burial or cremation?"

In an attempt to lighten things up, I say, "I have claustrophobia so I'd go with cremation."

"That's not funny, Jack. Honestly, if you survive, I might just kill you myself and be done with it."

"Fair enough," I say, which is obviously not the response she is looking for because there is not a lot of conversation during the rest of the meal, or on the drive home, and there is no dessert at her house either.

Back on my boat, I call Cubby at home to tell him what's going on. He already knows what I do about Alex Kramer and the Little League situation.

"Pick up a Kevlar vest at the station," he says. "But if you get a hole in it, I'll have to charge you for it."

"Sure, no problem, Cubby. Collect the cost from my estate."

"I can do that," he tells me. "By the way, are you leaving that cherry Vette to anyone in particular?"

This is the usual before-action cop banter, but Cubby does like my car, so it's not impossible he really wants to know.

"My will says that the car is to be sold and the proceeds donated to the Lee County Humane Society."

"That's a real shame, Jack. Good luck. And I was kidding about the vest."

But not about the car?

I get to the fruit stand at seven thirty to check out the location. Immokalee Road runs east of US 41 in Naples into farm country, with orange groves and fields of wheat, alfalfa, hay, potatoes, and soybeans. It is a very poor area, with tracts of run-down migrant worker housing.

The fruit stand is located about ten miles south of the town of Immokalee, with a dirt road running through the orange grove to a barn. The owner of the grove and his wife, both of whom I've met, live in a house about ten miles away from the property, so no one will be around except the occasional passing car.

Not for the first time, I'm operating out of my jurisdiction. Wade Hansen was the Naples police chief when I solved his serial killer case. Now he's the mayor. I called to tell him what I was up to within his city limits. He said, "That's fine, Jack. Just clean up your mess."

I park back near the barn, check my Smith & Wesson, and sit watching for headlights. In addition to the Kevlar vest, I'm wearing a wire from Fort Myers Beach PD, hoping to record Kramer's confession. That kind of recording does not require his consent. Obviously he does not intend to give me thirty thousand dollars. It's unlikely a fishing guide has that kind of cash on hand. If he's guilty, he intends to kill me. If not, we'll have an interesting conversation about Little League baseball.

By eight o'clock, Kramer has not shown up. By eight thirty, still no Kramer. I'm about to pack it in when I see the headlights of a truck coming up Immokalee Road. The truck is moving slowly. It passes the fruit stand, slows, backs up, turns onto the dirt road, and stops.

I see Kramer get out of the truck and look around. I turn on my headlights, get out of my car, and shout, "Walk toward me and bring the cash. No gun."

He gets out of the truck holding a white canvas boat bag. It doesn't take Sherlock Holmes to conclude that the bag contains a gun, not cash. I'm holding my S&W along my right leg.

He starts walking toward me. He's taking a big chance here, but he probably assumes I'm some jamoke trying for a big score who he can handle easily.

When he's twenty yards away I say, "Far enough."

He stops and says, "So what's the next move?"

"You're going to put that bag on the ground and drive away. If it contains thirty thousand dollars, you'll never hear from me again. If not, expect the police to come calling."

"How do I know you won't keep asking for more?"

"Because I know you're a killer and it's never a good idea to get on a killer's bad side."

"Got that right," he says, smiling in the headlight beams.

"First tell me, was it worth it, killing the Hendersons, just so your son could get more playing time?"

"It wasn't just the baseball thing. That fuckstick Larry Henderson thought he was hot shit, being a bank president. When I tried to talk to him about my son, he blew me off like I was a nobody. To guys like him, people like me don't exist."

"Well, you sure taught him a lesson. Too bad about his wife though."

"Collateral damage," he says.

I've now got enough on tape to convict him. But I'm making the mistake of thinking about that and not watching him closely enough as he reaches into the boat bag, comes out with a gun, and says, "Here's your cash, dipshit," as he fires a round right at me.

The bullet hits me center mass, a pretty good shot with the headlights in his eyes. The impact on my vest knocks me over backward. I roll to my left and as I am about to shoot, his head explodes in a red mist. He sinks to his knees, then topples to the ground.

I look behind me, where the shot came from. A man is standing at a door on the second floor of the barn, the place where hay bales are loaded into the loft. He's holding a rifle.

He waves and I wave back. I hear sirens coming down the road and see Cubby Cullen's SUV turn into the dirt road, followed by two cruisers. Cubby drives around Kramer's truck, parks near my car, gets out, and says, "I hope no one hit that Vette."

"Your sniper's a pretty good shot, Cubby."

He looks at the barn. "That's what, maybe fifty yards? Piece of cake for Tony. He wins the Florida Law Enforcement sharpshooter tournament every year."

"I had him myself," I say. "But thanks for setting up your man."

"Of course you had him, Jack. Not that it matters now, but did you get a confession on tape?"

"I did."

He comes over, taps me on the chest, and says, "I told you about damaging my vest."

It hurts. I'll have a major bruise there. "Take it out of my pay," I tell Cubby.

Police reports are public records. When a story about Alex Kramer killing the Hendersons appears in the *Fort Myers News-Press*, the national news media instantly goes into a viral feeding frenzy, equating the Little League angle to the Texas cheerleading moms.

I want no part of that, so Cubby agrees to do all the interviews. He looks pretty spiffy in his dress uniform while appearing remotely on all of the cable and network news shows. Cubby cites the excellent detective work done by his department, with the assistance of an unnamed "consultant." He's redacted my name from my report.

I'm fifty-one dollars to the good for my work with Fort Myers Beach PD—my one-dollar salary plus the fifty-dollar chip the slot-machine woman gave me in the Immokalee Casino. I spend the money wisely, by taking Marisa to dinner at the Veranda, that nice restaurant in Fort Myers favored by Lance Porter and Vivian Tolliver. I don't tell her that Alex Kramer shot me. Why spoil such a pleasant evening?

43.

A (Relatively) Happy Ending

A story that begins with two dead bodies found on a sailboat drifting in Pine Island Sound cannot have a completely happy ending. All I can do is report where things stand at the end of this story and let you decide if the taxpayers of Fort Myers Beach got their money's worth from this retired homicide detective.

I'm not Sherlock Holmes or Jack Stoney, both of whom solve cases by brilliant detective work, and both of whom are fictional characters. In the real world, most cases are solved using informants, or, when the perp confesses, which does happen, sometimes.

Oil Patch is nearing completion of its deep-water drilling platform in the gulf, due east of Fort Myers and right at the new fifty-mile coastal limit. News coverage of the project is mostly positive, given that two hundred jobs have been created and that a number of Florida construction companies are making sizable revenues building the rig. Sergey Pavlov's ownership of Oil Patch has not been discovered, and I see no reason to out him. Why make an enemy of a friend of Vladimir Putin?

Citizens for a Sane Environment is alleging that Oil Patch plans to use fracking to extract the gulf oil. The company denies that. I hear that the controversy is good for the Citizens fund-raising effort.

Lance Porter is still serving his time in the Union Correctional Institution. If I wanted him to, Cubby Cullen could use his law enforcement connections to check up on how Porter is doing, including what job he's been given and who his cellmate is. But I'd rather imagine the worst for that scumbag.

Lawrence and Marion Henderson's children, Nathan and Elise, were adopted by Larry's brother, Tom, and his wife, Lynette. I attended Nathan's ninth birthday party, held at one of those bounce houses in Fort Myers. After a trip to my chiropractor the next day I felt just fine.

Dr. Mitchell Gordon is expected to be elected and there's talk he'll be appointed to several key committees in the Florida House of Representatives when he is. He has a high approval rating, is respected by legislative members on both sides of the aisle, and everyone says he has a bright future in politics.

Chester Kravitz, principal owner of the Top Hat Casino in Atlantic City, was arrested by the FBI and charged with the theft of the Arrowhead Casino's money. All of Arrowhead's funds have been returned to the casino's account. Sarah Caldwell was able to get a search warrant, and the money trail led right to him.

Stoney's Dilemma, the Bill Stevens novel I edited, debuted at number one on the *New York Times* best-seller list, as have all the books in the series.

The son who said that the Manatee National Bank would regret repossessing his father's fishing boat, because the father was killed a few years ago by a sheriff's deputy during a gunfight, made good on his promise. He walked into a branch bank with a gun and got away with five thousand dollars from the teller drawers, making no effort to hide his identity from the security cameras. Then he robbed four more branches throughout the region over the next several months while hiding out. The robberies stopped. The son was never apprehended. In the old days, he might also have taken armloads of clock radios and stadium blankets.

Business is good at The Drunken Parrot and at the Arrowhead Casino. I knew a guy in Chicago who owned a grocery store. He always said that, whether times are good or times are bad, people gotta eat. It seems that the same is true about drinking and gambling.

Happiness is relative. You find it wherever you can, whenever you can, and enjoy it while you can. That's all any of us can do and, if we're lucky, it's enough.

44.

Eileen

Eileen was no lady.

It was September. By the time Marisa, who *was* a lady, and I decided to gather up a few irreplaceable possessions, including my cat, Joe, and evacuate from our homes in Fort Myers Beach, a small town on a barrier island off Florida's Southwest Gulf Coast, it was too late.

I blame the National Hurricane Center in Miami for misleading us. Gotta blame someone other than my own stupidity.

Eileen began as a tropical depression in the Caribbean and quickly spun up into a named tropical storm and then upped the ante into a Category 1, then a 2, and 3, and then a 4, and finally a killer 5 as it headed on a northwesterly track, causing catastrophic devastation to the Virgin Islands, Hispaniola, and the southern coast of Puerto Rico before it was predicted to jog northeast toward Florida's east coast, and then straight north toward coastal Georgia and the Carolinas.

It was truly a monster storm, the largest and most powerful in modern history, growing into "the size of France," the chief meteorologist at the Weather Channel said. Marisa was worried that the storm would hit Cuba, where she had friends and relatives, but it was the agreement of the American and European tracking models that it would not.

At my bar, The Drunken Parrot, all of the big-screen TVs remained tuned to CNN and the Weather Channel as we tracked Eileen's progress. We felt sympathy for those in the way, and relief that we would apparently not be among them.

Governor Anderson was on TV stating that Eileen would cause "massive devastation" wherever it made landfall and declaring a mandatory evacuation for Florida's east coast. The wait in lines at gas stations was already three hours long when the evacuation was ordered, with supplies depleting, and I-95, the only highway from Miami to Maine, turning into a parking lot.

On Wednesday, the Weather Channel told us that Eileen was likely to impact Florida's east coast on Sunday. No sweat. A day at the beach for Fort Meyers Beach.

I woke up Friday morning, turned on Mr. Coffee, slid a strawberry Pop-Tart into the toaster, opened a can of tuna for Joe, and punched the power On button on my galley TV's remote. I was shocked and awed to find that Eileen had altered its course. It was now heading toward Cuba and then projected to impact the Keys and the southwest Gulf Coast late Saturday or early Sunday as a powerful Cat 4.

Oops.

As I was finishing my Pop-Tart and pondering my dilemma, I heard a voice cry out, "Somali pirates! Prepare to be boarded!"

As far as I knew, there were no Somali pirates in Estero Bay. A thud hit the deck and *Phoenix* tilted to port. It was my pal Cubby Cullen, the town's porcine police chief. He came through the door into the main cabin and said, "Is the coffee still hot?" Without waiting for an answer, he found a mug in the cupboard.

"I'd think that '63 Corvette of yours could outrun the storm, Jack, but you should hit the road post-haste."

"Joe and I would go with Marisa in her Range Rover, but I imagine that I-75 is already jammed up and we wouldn't want Eileen to blow right up our tailpipe."

He sat at the galley table with his coffee and said, "Well, then, you all are welcome to shelter at the Lee County Public Safety Center on the mainland. It's built to withstand a Cat 5."

"We'll take you up on that," I said. "With my undying gratitude."

"Will there be enough gratitude left over to help with another homicide case?" he asked, knowing that, even without his hospitality during the storm, the answer would be yes.

I refilled my coffee cup, took a seat at the table and asked, "What've you got?"

He looked at his watch. "I've got a lot to do before the storm hits, so I'll give you the executive summary now and more detail later."

I had a lot to do too. I had to find a safe place for my car, then go to my bar and to Marisa's house and office to help her prepare. We had lots of bottled water at the bar and I had enough batteries for my flashlights and lanterns to handle the inevitable power outage and breakdown of other municipal services, post-storm. If the hurricane hit our little island head on as anything more than a Category 2, as it now seemed it would, there wasn't much chance that my houseboat or waterfront bar would survive the wind and storm surge. But, as they said in the marines, you prepare for the worst and hope for the best. In the corps, it always seemed to be the worst.

"Ever heard of Henry Wilberforce?" Cubby asked.

"You mean the rich old guy who lives in Naples?"

"Henry was probably the richest of the rich," Cubby said.

"Was, as in no longer alive, I take it."

"Correct."

"And, I also assume, he died of other than natural causes, or you wouldn't be telling me, a former homicide detective, about it."

"Also correct."

"Naples isn't in your jurisdiction, Cubby. They have their own police force, with their own detectives."

"The Naples police chief is a friend of mine. He called to ask if I knew of anyone with substantial experience in murder investigations because his detectives rarely catch a homicide and, as far as homicides go, this one's a doozy. I told him about you and volunteered you to take a look at the case file and to give an opinion. Given that we all survive the hurricane, of course."

"You will recall that, twice now, you've asked me to just take a look at a murder book and offer an opinion, and that I ended up doing far more than that. Including a case in Naples under a previous police chief."

"You don't play golf," Cubby said. "And your bartender mostly runs The Drunken Parrot, so what else have you got to do with your spare time?"

He had me there.

"When the storm passes, I'll have a cup of coffee with your pal," I told Cubby. "But I'm not promising more than that."

"Fair enough," Cubby said. Then he left to organize his department's storm preparations, including ensuring that everyone who'd not evacuated could get to a shelter over the causeway on the mainland.

I called Marisa and said, "Hi, this is your first responder. Do you require assistance?"

"I'm scared shitless, Jack. We should have headed north. What should we do?"

I could tell she was frightened because she never had used language like that before.

"Cubby Cullen was just here. We can shelter in the public service building. Hang tight for the moment. Sam and I will board up the bar's windows then be over to do that to your properties."

"What about your boat?" she asked.

"If Eileen wants it, she can have it," I answered. "To try to secure it would be like rearranging the deck chairs on the Titanic."

Marisa lived on Mango Street in a pink stucco cottage with a green tin roof. Her three-agent real estate office was downtown on Estero Boulevard in a one-story, white concrete block building that also housed an insurance agency and a dentist's office. The insurance agency was going to be a busy place come Monday, if it was still there.

Joe finished his tuna and meowed at me. "Don't worry, buddy, I won't forget you," I told him as I scratched his head. "You're going with me to the shelter."

Saturday morning, with Eileen scheduled to arrive sometime Sunday afternoon, the TV weather people were warning, as they always did, that the storm could still turn this way or that and end up farther west before heading north into the Gulf of Mexico, threatening the Florida Panhandle, or Mississippi, or Louisiana.

When I pulled my Vette into the bar's coquina-shell parking lot, Sam already was up on a ladder screwing plywood onto the windows.

"Thought you'd be in Chicago by now, boss," he said.

"Didn't want to miss the excitement, Sam. You have somewhere to go before the hurricane arrives?"

"I'll be at the casino with friends and family. It's built to last."

Sam and I spent the next two hours boarding up the windows, putting anything breakable, including liquor, beer bottles, and dishes, into cardboard boxes, and securing anything outside that we could. The tiki bar, like my boat, would be left to the storm. Maybe it would end up in Atlanta. Then we drove in Sam's Ford F-150 truck to Marisa's house. Later I'd find somewhere to shelter my Vette.

Saturday afternoon, time to cross the Matanzas Pass Bridge from Estero Island onto the mainland. I was driving Marisa's Range Rover, containing her and Joe, plus our important papers, my gun collection, her jewelry, family pictures, and selected clothing. Cubby told us we wouldn't need food or bottled water because the Lee County Public Safety Center had plenty of both.

When we arrived at the two-story, concrete-block building, the parking lot was full of cars and trucks, police, fire department, and Red Cross vehicles, EMT vans, and boats on trailers. The center had been designated as a staging area for first responders who would deal with Eileen's aftermath. A garage used to store equipment was set up to shelter pets. Joe didn't consider himself to be a pet, so I'd ask permission to have him inside with us in his carrier.

Pending that permission, I left Joe in the Range Rover as Marisa and I carried our baggage into the building. A female Lee County sheriff's deputy checked us in at a table at the entrance to a large auditorium which had been set up with cots and bedding. I hoped that the deputy was a cat person, which she was, telling me that I could bring Joe in as long as he stayed in his carrier, which was large enough to accommodate his litter box and food and water dishes.

The center had a large kitchen and dining room where coffee and sandwiches were being served. So far, some four hundred people had checked into the shelter, with more expected. When it was full, people would be directed to other shelters, including Germaine Arena, where hockey games, rodeos, circuses, and concerts were held. Florida state and local governments knew how to prepare for hurricanes.

Marisa and I picked out two cots along a wall and I went back out to the Ranger Rover to retrieve Joe. I put his crate on my cot and joined Marisa in the cafeteria where we had coffee and ham sandwiches and chatted with our shelter mates. There was a sense of community in the place, of shared danger and determination to endure whatever hardships were in store for us, and to do whatever necessary to rebuild our post-hurricane lives, whatever they might be.

Every area of the country had its own brand of natural disaster—fires and earthquakes on the west coast, tornadoes in the Midwest, and hurricanes on the east coast. Blizzards during northern winters, and flooding from rivers. So there was nowhere you could live to hide from Mother Nature. At least with hurricanes, you got plenty of warning. Unless, of course, the track of the storm abruptly shifted, as had happened to us. As they said in the marines, sometimes there was nothing to do but bend over and kiss your ass good-bye.

We awoke Sunday morning to two pieces of good luck: the Lee County shelter staff was making pancakes, waffles, eggs, bacon, and sausages for breakfast; and the hurricane was tracking farther west, up the middle of the gulf, heading toward the panhandle. Heavy rain, high winds, and the possibility of tornadoes were predicted for our neck of the woods, but not the devastating storm with flooding we were expecting.

Dodged the bullet. I had dodged real bullets during my military and police career, but this reprieve felt just as fortunate.

Marisa and I had a nice breakfast, passed on lunch, and by three P.M. we grabbed our duffle bags and Joe in his cage and left the shelter.

Back at Marisa's house, we watched cable news as Eileen slammed into a wide area of the panhandle. including the towns of Destin, Fort Walton Beach, and Gulf Breeze as a Cat 2, causing flooding and extensive wind damage to coastal buildings and trees. First responders and emergency crews gathered at our shelter headed north to help deal with the aftermath. On the way home, we drove through some flooded streets and around downed trees across roads. Electrical power was out in some areas, but not in Marisa's neighborhood, and the county government advised boiling drinking water. With only those problems to deal with, we considered ourselves lucky.

"Is it wrong to feel happy that the main storm missed us when it damaged other towns?" Marisa asked me as she was preparing one of her gourmet Cuban dinners.

"That's a philosophical conundrum," I answered. "Churchill said, 'There is nothing so exhilarating as to be shot at without result.' But I'm certain he didn't want someone else to be hit by a bullet intended for him. All we can do at this point is to enjoy your nice dinner and make a donation to the Red Cross." Both of which we did.

By Thursday, the power was on all over Lee County, the roads were dry, the downed trees were off the streets, and water could be used right out of the faucets. Life was back to normal.

Or at least it was until I had lunch with Cubby Cullen to hear more about the Naples murder investigation.

Cubby and I met for lunch at Captain Mack's Seafood Shack on the Caloosahatchee River. I found him sitting outside on the deck overlooking the river, enjoying a bowl of clam chowder. An osprey dove for a fish and came up with one—his own lunch.

"You know the rule," Cubby said as I slid onto a bench at the booth. "Whoever gets here first is allowed to start eating."

I looked at my watch. "I'm right on time, Cubby."

"As my first boss at the Toledo Police Department said, on time is ten minutes late."

The waitress came to take my order and the rest of Cubby's. We'd both been to Captain Mack's so often that we didn't need menus. I asked for the chowder and we both added fried clam strip rolls and onion rings. Captain Mack had been a tuna boat captain in Massachusetts. When Japanese fleets overfished the waters, he sold his boat and moved to Florida with his wife to open an authentic New England seafood restaurant. I always went for the clam strips rather than the whole bellies. Bite into a whole belly clam and a greenish-brown substance oozes out. Know what that is? Clam poop. None for me, thanks.

I asked Cubby about the Naples murder case.

"As I said, the deceased was an eighty-two-year-old man named Henry Wilberforce III. He was found in bed by his butler with a gunshot wound in his forehead. He lived in Lake Forest, outside Chicago, with a winter home in Naples. He was the heir to the Wilberforce Food Company fortune. That's a Chicago company you may recognize."

Being from Chicago, I did. A great many of the food items found on supermarket shelves were produced by Wilberforce Foods.

"Any leads about who might have shot him?"

"I'd rather have you hear that directly from Naples Police Chief Tom Sullivan. I owe him a favor. He's expecting your call."

Our food arrived. I didn't ask Cubby why he owed Sullivan a favor. I assumed it was confidential or he would have told me. I said, "Fine, I'll call Sullivan this afternoon."

I did call him, and what happened next is another story entirely.

Acknowledgments

The Permanent Press in Sag Harbor, New York, has now published three of my novels. Many thanks to them for that. Co-publishers Marty and Judy Shepard and Chris Knopf, and copy editor Barbara Anderson all contributed skillful editing, somehow finding a readable book in the mountain of manuscript pages I delivered to them. Once again, designer Lon Kirschner has created a first-class cover.

When I attended Hamilton College in Clinton, New York, every freshman was required to take a course in expository writing. We had to undergo a series of tests each semester (I don't recall how many) which involved sitting in a classroom with a blue book and pen and writing an essay on a given topic. There were only two grades: "Yes" and "No." To get a "Yes," everything had to be absolutely perfect: grammar, spelling, punctuation, the logic of your argument, and whatever else the professor deemed to constitute a good essay according to the rules set forth by Strunk and White's *The Elements of Style*. This was before the age of word processing, computerized spelling and grammar checking, and Google and Siri to help you out. You had to get three "Yes" themes each semester to pass the course. I remember the premed students, especially, sweating this out; you couldn't get into medical school with an F on your transcript. I never knew of anyone not to pass the course, but some had to wait until the last test to get that third "Yes." Every time I hear from a publisher that it wants one of my books, I feel like I've just gotten another "Yes" theme and that, a half-century removed from College Hill, still feels very good, indeed.

I would be remiss to not mention that, after the story ends in September of 2016, Jack Starkey's beloved Chicago Cubs went on to win the World Series by beating the Cleveland Indians in game 7, 8 to 7. The Cubbies had appeared in eleven World Series, their last victories coming by winning back-to-back titles in 1907 and 1908. So it had been a long time, 108 years precisely, since the boys put on championship rings. Jack was there, watching the game on the roof of Bill Stevens's apartment building, one of those Wrigley Rooftops, which are residential buildings near Wrigley Field with bleachers on their roofs providing a view of the games. Marisa was invited, but she had to stay home to close the sale of a multimillion-dollar house, this causing Jack to seriously question her priorities.